A whirlwind romance in Paris had led in no time to Laura marrying the devastating Karl Rievenbeck—and not until she married him did she realise that he was devastatingly rich as well. Then he took her to his luxurious home in Italy, and she discovered the fly in the ointment— in the person of the glamorous Contessa Eleanora Ferrara . . .

DIVINE RIGHT

BY

ANN COOPER

MILLS & BOON LIMITED
15–16 BROOK'S MEWS
LONDON W1A 1DR

First published 1983
Australian copyright 1983
Philippine copyright 1983
This edition 1983

© Ann Cooper

ISBN 0 263 74329 2

Set in Monophoto Times 10 on 10 pt.
01–0983 – 61566

Made and printed in Great Britain by
Richard Clay (The Chaucer Press) Ltd,
Bungay, Suffolk

CHAPTER ONE

'BEAUTIFUL . . .' There was an interesting accent tucked into the man's dark brown voice, and Laura instinctively knew he wasn't referring to the Mona Lisa. Her back stiffened as she glanced over her shoulder.

'I believe one or two people have remarked on that before now,' she said, her cool green eyes quelling further comment. However, the wretched man wasn't put off.

'You were here yesterday,' he said, again in English. How had he known she was English?

'Very observant of you,' she said, resuming her study of the painting, aware that a security guard was watching them. Why didn't he go away? Who was he anyway? He wasn't French. What then? German, Austrian, Swiss? . . . Not that she cared in the slightest.

'You like paintings?' he tried again, and his accent was more pronounced this time, more fractured—sexier; she believed he had done it on purpose.

Laura cast him a covert glance out of the corner of her eye. Not bad—if you went in for the urbane sophistication of European businessmen. She preferred the more artistic type, herself.

He was waiting for her answer, for a moment she had difficulty recalling the question. 'Do I like paintings?' she repeated with a shrug. 'Some.' She wasn't telling him that she was determined to become a top illustrator one day.

'Whenever I am in Paris I come always to the Louvre,' he said, his blue eyes warming as they flicked over her. 'You are here on holiday, yes?' he added.

'No,' she said firmly, removing the sunglasses from the top of her head and snapping them down on her nose. 'Now, if you'll excuse me,' and she brushed past him, catching a faint tang of his expensive cologne. She felt her skin prickle and her shoulder blades tightened as she forced herself to stroll out of the gallery. She knew he watched her all the way, her cool green and white sundress and high-heeled sandals accentuating long legs and a slim yet shapely figure. Somehow she managed to wait until she was out of his sight before attempting to pat a few short honey-coloured curls into place. Her usually friendly smile was tempered into a firm, disapproving line. Men like that always looked at a woman as if she was theirs by right. Well, this was one pick-up that hadn't worked. But, curiously, there was no satisfaction in the thought . . .

For some reason, Laura still felt strung up about the man as she let herself into the little fourth-floor flat. The other girls were all out on Saturday morning shopping sprees and for once she was pleased to have the place to herself. It was hot, stuffy, and she went around opening windows; maybe she would sunbathe out on the roof after lunch. Then, wondering if there was any homemade lemonade left, she went through to the little kitchen and saw a couple of letters on the table. They were both for her, one from a friend in the same year as her at college who was spending the summer holidays in America, and the other was a bill. . . . Still nothing from Anthea. Maybe Laura ought to phone London over the weekend. Her stepmother hadn't been this late sending her allowance before.

There was some lemonade, and she poured herself a glass; phew, that was better! She didn't normally feel the heat like this. It was that man's fault, somehow he had really got under her skin. Usually she could give men the brush-off or keep them easily at arm's length, like she did the two or three fellows interested in her at the moment; what was it about the man in the Louvre that made her feel different?

Refusing to think about him any more, Laura put on her bikini, and took some cheese and an apple and her sketch pad out on to the roof. It was quite safe, she could climb out of her bedroom window and be surrounded by dormer windows without even a peep of the street way, way below. There was a flat area just large enough to stretch out her towel, and then with a cushion propped against the slope of the roof, she could sit almost upright and sketch away happily for hours . . .

What was it about that man . . .? Purely as a drawing exercise, of course, Laura began sketching little cameos. . . . His head and shoulders, somehow catching the uplift of his lips when he had smiled quizzically at her. And another one showing the cut of his smooth dark hair as it curved around his ear; funny how she could remember so much about the man after one very short meeting; it was obviously her professional artist's eye! The page was rapidly filling; at the top was his firm profile, and tucked into an odd space was his full face as he had smiled down at her, those blue eyes taunting and sexy. In a few skilful lines she had caught the lethal essence of the man, the tall, masculine shape hinting at a virile aggression lying dormant—waiting. How did she know that? Laura felt her palms go damp; maybe she had drawn enough. So she put her pad aside and stretched out on her towel, rolling over on to her stomach and undoing the fastening of her bikini bra— not that she really needed to wear one out here; no one could see her. How good the sun felt! She mustn't get burnt, but maybe if she just closed her eyes a moment she could forget all about him . . . And a few moments later she drifted into a warm, sensual haze and somehow she heard the soft sexy accent of someone whispering, 'Beautiful.'

She saw him again, as easily as that, and her eyes were still closed, she didn't even need her sketches. She saw the strong attractive lines of his face as he had looked down at her. Which meant he had been tall— very tall. His eyes were blue, yes, and she could see the way the corners of his sensuous mouth had curved upwards. She wriggled into her towel, a little insect

scurried across her damp back, but she didn't have the
heart to brush it away. Supposing he was here now—
whatever his name was. She imagined his smooth palm
sliding down her hip ... her thighs. She stretched
luxuriously and her toes curled ... Then someone was
shouting her name, one of the girls was back and did
Laura want to go to a party? Of course she did, and
thank goodness to be disturbed from such outrageous
thoughts!

But somehow the evening didn't turn out as exciting
as usual. Laura stood for a moment, drink in one hand,
watching everyone dancing, the room thick with smoke
and heavy with music ... and somehow ... somehow
something was missing.

The crowd had arranged a day out on Sunday and it
was normally the kind of trip Laura would have loved
to join. But she made an excuse of finishing off her
canvas. 'I've arranged to start my painting on Monday,'
she told Colette, whose flat it was, and who worked in
an advertising agency. Colette attended the art college
on a part-time basis and that was how Laura had met
her, when the older girl had advertised a room to let in
her flat. But really, today she just felt the need to have a
quiet day on her own. She felt restless. She would
phone Anthea and find out why her stepmother hadn't
sent any money lately—or answered her two letters.
Luckily she had managed to save quite a bit of her
allowance, so her rent was safe for the next few weeks—
but what about after that?

She phoned mid-morning when she guessed Anthea
would be up. But there was no reply ... Laura frowned,
wondering if there was something really wrong. Of
course not, bad news always travelled fast.

Putting the phone down, she padded back to her
room on bare feet. It was hot again today, too hot to
stay indoors—maybe she could take her sketch pad
down to the Seine, it was one of her favourite spots.

Normally, she would have had lunch out, but caution
made her economise, so she put together some biscuits,

cheese and salady things, and poured the rest of the lemonade into a flask with some ice cubes.

She pottered about happily, loving the little flat and realising how fortunate she was to be here. She could still remember the excitement when her father had agreed that she could come to Paris. *Paris!* What a dream! What an opportunity! And really, it had been better for her to leave home, because he had, then, recently married Anthea, and they could hardly have wanted a grown-up daughter around.

Laura perched on the edge of the table and stared sadly at the sloping ceiling. But all that had been fifteen months ago—just before he had had his stroke. Although he had still insisted that she come to Paris—and by the November he had been dead. Christmas had been dreadful, and she had wondered if Anthea would allow her to come back to Paris—but her stepmother had been adamant, and by February, when Laura had telephoned one weekend, the phone had been answered by a man . . . Laura couldn't understand how Anthea could turn to someone else so quickly. And by the time the Easter holidays had come round it was pretty obvious that Anthea had more than one man in line.

Now she sighed, and put the bits and pieces back into the fridge. That was why she had decided to stay in Paris for the long summer vacation. If she went home she and Anthea would only fight.

Yet the problem of the money still had to be sorted out. She went through to the living room and phoned again. Still no reply. She would have to try later.

It was a pleasant walk through the hot, deserted Sunday back streets. Laura carried her lunch and sketching things in a colourful raffia basket. Today she was wearing a cool blue cotton skirt and low, V-neck, blue and white tee-shirt. Yesterday's high, spiky sandals had been exchanged for comfortable espadrilles. Her short, honey-coloured curls bounced to their own tune as she had come to realise they always would. Large, owlish sunglasses completed her casual outfit. Today she would enjoy herself without the aggravation of menacing men.

Her sketch pad filled rapidly. She settled herself upstream from one of the bridges, near where the Touring Club of France had visitors' moorings. Yachts, with masts lashed horizontally to their decks, nestled and nudged between large and small cabin cruisers, all of them carrying the flags of different nations. There was a large man smoking a pipe; Laura quickly transferred him to paper; a girl pegging washing on a tiny plastic line; a German family all in shorts or bikinis just about to set out lunch . . . Time passed and Laura's fingers couldn't work quickly enough. Next came the bridge, with its arches, columns, sculptured figures and gold ornamentation . . . it really was beautiful . . . Barges, large greenhouse pleasure-boats filled with tourists, floating restaurants . . . work-boats . . . Laura captured it all, page after page of people, boats, the sun glistening on the river . . . the large grey buildings on the other side where, today, traffic was tearing along the one-way system that would get snarled up in the weekday rush . . .

People came and drifted away, staying for a while to watch her work. Some Americans spoke to her and she was pleased to talk. How long had she been in Paris? Wasn't she the luckiest girl in the world? As Laura strolled home that evening, she rather thought she was.

There was still no reply from London when she phoned Anthea again. Perhaps she had gone away for the weekend. Laura tried to push the problem out of her mind as she went and prepared an omelette and salad supper. But there was still no letter and cheque from London the following morning as she rushed through breakfast. At last she was ready. What a good thing the other girls had gone off to work earlier, because at the moment the place seemed to be full of her own clutter! *Whose turn is it to clean the bathroom?* she scribbled on the blackboard next to the cooker. Sometimes the girls didn't see each other for a whole week; they passed like ships in the night, their only means of communication a piece of chalk.

Still worrying about Anthea, Laura struggled down the narrow, twisting stairs with the paints, easel and large piece of hardboard. Could she splash out on a taxi? By the time she reached the street she decided such extravagance would be essential.

Anthea was forgotten as the taxi pulled up outside the Louvre. Laura was excited. This was the first time she had been to an art gallery to copy one of the Old Masters. Most students didn't bother these days—such a thing was out of fashion. But she had wanted to do it—and her art teacher was one of the old school, and had said it would be a good experience for her to try and discover how they had achieved their colours. Only by actually painting was it possible to discover their techniques. Not that Laura saw herself as such an old-fashioned painter. She wanted to illustrate, preferably children's books. But it was all a question of experience, painting, painting, painting; discovering and perfecting her own technique.

She had chosen to copy *The Forge* by Le Nain Although her teacher had said that a true copy was impossible, Laura was hoping to prove him wrong.

One of the gallery assistants was ready for her, and he helped her spread out a giant sheet of canvas to protect the highly polished floor. It was still early, the gallery almost empty, as she set up her easel and someone found her a high stool on which to rest her paintbox. Not that she would get round to much painting today; the canvas was already prepared and marked out in squares; her first job was to sketch roughly the positions of the figures . . .

She was totally absorbed as she worked, wearing an old, much splattered smock over her tee-shirt and jeans. The picture was seventeenth-century, French—all browns, creams and ochres with splashes of sienna. It was the interior of a forge, showing three generations of a peasant family, the glow from the furnace highlighting their forms, while casting sombre shadows all around. It was a strong picture, vital; to her, expressing latent power and stability at the heart of a people who had then been suppressed by an *ancien régime* and its adherence to absolutism.

She sketched the outline of the blacksmith ... his wife ... the old father sitting in a corner, no longer capable of heavy work, yet comforting one of the children who looked a little afraid of the fire ... Laura worked without thought of time, or the one or two people who strolled into the gallery and watched her working. She was getting used to that. She had been painting seriously for over five years now. Her father had said it was a pity her mother hadn't lived to see it. Not that Laura could remember her mother, she had died when Laura had been a few months old ...

At last she stood back and surveyed her work. Not bad—not good; the angle of the anvil wasn't quite right ... and through her absorption came the sound of slow footsteps. One ... two ... three ... Laura stared at her painting with unseeing eyes, but not for a million pounds would she have turned round. She picked up a brush and a piece of rag, fiddling with them, noticing that her hands were trembling.

'Beautiful,' he said again, he was right behind her now—and the Mona Lisa wasn't anywhere in sight.

Laura cleared her throat. 'Oh, it's you again,' she said, turning round in surprise, then picking up some paint and squirting it on to her palette—bother, far too much. She could feel his eyes on her, they really were as blue as she remembered. He was wearing another suit today, light grey, interestingly cut in the Continental fashion. Those shoes looked hand-sewn.

Intrigued in spite of herself, Laura glanced up at him, and their eyes met—held—her stomach flipped over, and she had to look away quickly, suddenly hot, breathless ...

'Are you a student here in Paris?' And as if reacting to her confusion his voice was almost matter-of-fact.

She continued mixing paint, trying to match the blacksmith's jacket—not that she was ready to do him yet . . .

'Or have you just come over here to work during the holiday?' he tried again, and she could smell his aftershave, sharp yet musky—discreet yet potently virile.

'I'm a student—here in Paris. I've been here nearly a year,' she said, more to stop her train of thought than to supply him with information. And because she had to get rid of him somehow, she added, 'Is this your usual lunchtime pick-up spot, or do you prowl around here all day?'

His lips twisted, anger then humour swiftly crossed the strong lines of his face. He looked very European— very confident. A slim, expensive briefcase was tucked casually under one arm. His smooth dark hair had little auburn flecks in it . . . Laura turned quickly away.

'Prowl?' He frowned innocently, rolling his r's in a seductive growl. 'Excuse me, what is—*prowl*?'

Laura shivered; lord, that *accent*!

'Pick-up—chase—pursue,' she said, a little too loudly, and the security guard over by the doorway looked across at her and smiled.

'Ah!' Enlightenment dawned. 'Yes, I—*prowl.*' Again he made a meal of it, sounding like a dangerous, predatory cat. 'But only when I see something I want— something I want very much.' And again their eyes met, and held—and Laura felt panic and excitement mingled with cold hard anger.

'Will you go away and leave me alone!' she hissed, glancing significantly at the guard, but he was talking to a group of tourists now. It wasn't easy having an argument in an art gallery; like in a library, you instinctively felt you ought to whisper.

'Don't be cross—come and have lunch with me.'

'Go to hell!'

His hands spread. 'Hell?'

'And don't start that again,' she snapped. 'You speak English as well as I do.'

'Coffee, then,' he persisted.

Laura waved a paintbrush at him. He took an immediate step back. 'Go away—leave me alone—or I'll have you arrested!'

He walked away—just like that. She turned back to her painting, suddenly crestfallen. One, two, three, the precise footsteps receded . . . then stopped. *Stopped!* Oh no! He had sat himself down on one of the hard leather settees provided for visitors who wanted to linger and gaze at the paintings. Only he wasn't gazing at the paintings, he was gazing at Laura. Never mind. She dabbed purposefully at the blacksmith's jacket. Bother, the colour wasn't a bit right . . . Ten minutes, twenty minutes . . . again she rubbed out her mistake with a rag . . . half an hour . . .

'Okay,' she said, laying down her brushes and palette and marching over to the settee, 'I'll have coffee with you—but *only* if you promise to leave me alone afterwards.'

He had the cheek to consider it, but at last he eased his tall, lethally masculine figure into a standing position. 'Very well, Miss Laura Grant, we shall have coffee, and afterwards . . .'

'How did you know my name?' she interrupted, her green eyes wide and incredulous in her bright elfin face.

A curious light flickered behind his eyes, then he led her back to the easel, his fingers burning her arm. And there, stencilled inside the open lid, was the name she had put there herself when her father had first given her the huge wooden box of paints years ago.

'Laura,' he said again, softly, almost to himself. No one had ever spoken her name quite like that before.

'Just coffee,' she reminded him, snapping the lid shut and putting her brushes into a jam-jar. 'Ten minutes—and then you leave.' And she picked up her shoulder bag and left everything else under the watchful eyes of the security guard. Normally she would have taken off her smock before going to have coffee—but it would do him good to be seen with a scruffy female for a change.

Something told her that a man like this usually went in for the sophisticated type. So why, she thought, is he bothering with me?

She had decided to sit in mutinous silence. Coffee, she had said, but hadn't mentioned anything about talking. Yet it wasn't easy; heads turned as they walked into the café, stylish women openly admiring him ... To be fair, he really was an attractive man ... Attractive? Handsome? Not exactly. As they threaded their way to a vacant table she tried to study him with the objective eye of a professional. He was strong, resourceful, masculine, virile ... these were the words that came to mind. The well cut business suit didn't disguise broad shoulders, a trim, firm stomach, long legs and narrow, lethal hips ... It all added up to a devastating image of potential danger. Only that really wasn't an *objective* assessment, was it?

'How did you know I was English—on Saturday, when you spoke to me?' she asked, because perhaps it would be better to talk about something; left alone her mind seemed to be heading along unacceptable lines.

'I heard you talking to one of the gallery assistants.' They had reached a table and he was drawing out a chair for her. 'Your French is about as good as mine.' His tone suggested he wasn't being complimentary to either of them, and Laura gritted her teeth. After eight weeks at a language school and then nine months at art college, she was beginning to think her grasp of the language was more than passable.

'Do you often come to Paris?' she said, when he had ordered their coffee and there was nothing to do but sit and wait for it.

'Several times a year. This time I am here until Friday.'

'Oh!' and she had to bite her tongue to stop from adding, 'Is that all?' 'Where do you come from? I—er—can't place the accent,' she added, self-conscious now and trying to sound extremely casual.

'I'm Italian.' And when she looked surprised, he

added. 'From Northern Italy—from an area that used
to belong to Austria. Many of us still speak German
. . .' and Laura presumed that was what accounted for
his unusual accent—it really did have an amazing effect
on her. Then he seemed to remember he hadn't
introduced himself, and with an annoyed little frown he
reached into his jacket and pulled out a business card.
'Rievenbeck,' he said, passing it across to her. 'Karl
Rievenbeck,' and there was a hint of what?—pride?—
caution?—almost as if he had expected her to recognise
his name.

Huh! She put down the card without looking at it.
Karl Rievenbeck. It suited him. Their coffee arrived
and he passed her the sugar. She took a couple of grains
on the end of her spoon and thoughtfully stirred them
into her cup. What manner of man was this Karl
Rievenbeck? Was he a hard, shrewd business man?
Obviously. But what else? Had he been aware of the stir
he had caused when he walked in here? He had
certainly *seemed* unaware, or did that prove he had had
plenty of practice at hiding it?

Laura kept stirring her coffee. Really, she shouldn't
be here, he wasn't her type. She thought of the men
in her life to date who all wore jeans and tee-shirts,
and if they had been sitting here now, they would all
be taken for students or tourists . . . But Karl
Rievenbeck would never fit into either of those
categories. He was way out of her class. Yet he
wasn't coming on strong with sexual overtones as she
had expected. Instead, as he reached for the sugar, he
asked her about her studies and what she hoped to
achieve, and she found herself smiling and chatting
quite naturally to him as he watched her carefully and
slowly piled three teaspoons of sugar into his
coffee—*three!*

'You were saying you want to illustrate children's
books.'

'What—oh, yes.' Laura dragged her mind back to the
conversation. 'I'm—er—gradually putting together a

portfolio. We give exhibitions at college and I've already sold one or two things.'

'I envy you,' he said, sipping his hot, *sweet* coffee. For a moment his face looked strange.

'I wouldn't want to do anything else,' she said, giving herself a mental shake. He really must have an extremely sweet tooth. And then he was asking her about the picture she was copying and she found herself telling him about the three Nain brothers ...

'How long will it take you?'

'I don't know—I haven't done a copy like this before.'

'So you'll be here tomorrow?'

She laughed. 'Good lord, yes—and next week; probably next month ...' and then she realised what he was getting at and her heart missed a beat, and in spite of herself she felt a tiny thrill that this sophisticated business man wanted to see her again.

'Then will you have lunch with me tomorrow?' The eyes were calm, but the accent was quietly seductive, and as she hesitated, a dark brow was raised in sardonic humour. 'Do not be afraid that I shall spirit you away for the whole afternoon. One hour only—and then I shall send you back to work.'

Laura grinned, and although it was all crazy and of course he was just amusing himself between business appointments, it couldn't really do any harm—and there did seem to be *something* in the air between them. 'Thank you,' she said, accepting his invitation graciously, 'but I'll be in my working clothes.'

'I'm sure that—given time—I shall learn to love the smell of ...' The word escaped him.

'Turpentine?' she suggested.

He nodded and they laughed, their eyes dancing together, and suddenly it was as if they had known each other for all time ... as if she had been waiting for this very moment. There was a blending, an empathy, and a deep, deep excitement stirring her soul. She was suddenly flustered and he immediately looked away, picking up their bill and organising payment. As he did so she surreptitiously slipped his card into the pocket of her smock. As they rose to leave she noticed that he had only drunk half his coffee.

'I let it get cold, listening to you,' he said. And when they were outside he took her hand in a formal little shake, adding, 'until tomorrow—Laura.'

She smiled a goodbye, then turned purposefully and walked along the other passageway, and she waited until she had returned to her gallery before hurriedly taking his card out of her pocket. Karl Rievenbeck, it said, and there were two addresses, one in Milan and one in Rome. His firm obviously had two branches, but their name wasn't on the card.

Slowly she slipped the card back in her pocket and picked up her brushes again ... Eventually she was absorbed and worked through until six o'clock before realising that she hadn't eaten all day.

She hurried home, by Métro this time, because the gallery was locking all her gear away in one of their cupboards. She ran up the stairs, whistling as she let herself into the little flat ... There was still no letter from Anthea.

'You sound cheerful,' said Colette, coming out of the bathroom with a towel wrapped round her head. 'Had a good day? Did the painting go well?'

'Oh yes, super, it's really working out very well,' Laura enthused, putting on the kettle and hungrily raiding the biscuit tin. And her painting was the reason for this light, bubbly mood, wasn't it? she thought, nibbling a custard cream. I mean, who in their right mind falls in love with a man simply because he puts three spoonsful of sugar in his coffee! Crazy, she laughed to herself—crazy!

CHAPTER TWO

LUNCH was a success. Laura had taken a chance and had worn a sprigged cotton skirt with a little white short-sleeved, Victorian-type blouse. At breakfast the girls had looked surprised, but Laura said that jeans were hot and she had found a long, loose overall as a giant cover-up. There was still no letter from Anthea, but she hardly gave it a thought as she travelled to the Louvre by Métro.

The morning didn't pass as quickly as before; she spent quite a bit of time glancing at her watch. But eventually it was one o'clock, and her heart lifted as she heard those familiar footsteps.

She turned to greet Karl Rievenbeck with a smile, but nothing had prepared her for the devastating change in his appearance. Gone were the formal business suit and attaché case; instead he was wearing immaculate oatmeal slacks, cut with skill to accentuate narrow hips and firm thighs ... The open-necked shirt casually moulded broad shoulders and a flat, athletically trim stomach. He had a Leica slung from one shoulder and a brown cord jacket slung over the other.

'Playing hookey?' Laura grinned, and then had to explain what that meant as they made their way to the restaurant.

'I don't have to work all the time,' he said, as they took their places. Today Laura had left her overall in the gallery, experience telling her that he liked her casual, feminine outfit.

'You look like a tourist,' she said unbelievably.

'I am. I'm going to persuade you to show me around. You must know Paris far better than I.'

'I can't.' Laura's green eyes widened. 'You promised

not to whisk me away—you said you would send me straight back to work.'

He accepted the wine list with a sigh. 'So I did—a pity.' He ordered and they were alone again, his eyes quietly serious. Lord, they really were the most terrific blue . . . 'Then I mustn't try and persuade you?'

'No.'

He nodded. 'Very well.'

Laura felt instantly disappointed.

'What about tomorrow, then? It's Wednesday tomorrow and I have a lot to achieve by Friday.'

She remembered with a sinking heart that he would be in Paris only three more days. 'You won't achieve much if you keep going sightseeing,' she said, but he only smiled a little smile to himself and said nothing. Laura picked up her fork and traced a pattern on the white tablecloth. Their hors d'oeuvres arrived. 'I suppose I could take a couple of hours off tomorrow.'

Karl's blue eyes shone. 'Why not all day? We'll go anywhere you choose. Come on, Laura,' his accent lingered over her name and she had to suppress a shiver. 'One day—that's all I need. To—er—relax from my work,' he added when she looked a bit surprised. 'I have a very heavy schedule.'

'Anywhere I choose?' she asked with a devilish grin.

'Anywhere.'

She stared at him thoughtfully. Where would a man like Karl Rievenbeck go on a day's relaxation? Did he really want to see the sights? Wouldn't lunch in an expensive restaurant be more his style? And an afternoon on the river, perhaps, and the evening spent in an elegant, exclusive night club.

'I know a very pretty little place on the river,' she began, trying to keep a straight face. 'It's quite a drive from here, the scenery is beautiful—but you have to climb up to the castle to see it properly. It's quite a hard climb,' she exaggerated, 'it would mean taking a picnic.'

She waited for his face to fall, but it didn't. 'Where is this place?' he asked instead.

'Les Andelys.'

'Ah!' To her surprise he seemed to know it. Then he reached across the table and lightly touched her hand. 'You make a good choice.' He frowned, his thumb absentmindedly caressing her fingers ... if he did it much longer she would drop the fork. 'Andelys,' he repeated, 'Petit Andelys?' and when she nodded, because her throat was suddenly constricted, he smiled a smile that did wonderful things for the strong lines of his face. 'I have a friend who has a boat moored there. Perhaps we could have our picnic on the river? Anchor somewhere? Go for a swim ...?'

At last he gave her back her hand—luckily Laura used the other one to pick up her glass of wine. 'I'm not a very good swimmer,' she admitted, taking a sip.

'Then we will have just the picnic,' he assured her quickly, settling back in his chair quite enthusiastically. 'I haven't been on a picnic for years.'

It was a chastening reminder that he didn't normally wear oatmeal slacks and casual shirts ... and for the umpteenth time Laura wondered what such an international businessman could want with a little nobody like herself.

She gave him her address; he said he would collect her early the next morning, and then they settled down to their meal ... yet it wasn't until she was on her way home that evening that she realised she still didn't know where Karl Rievenbeck was staying. Come to that, she didn't know anything about him at all. Except that his part of Italy had once been in Austria—but that didn't tell you much about a man, did it?

But there were some things it wasn't necessary to know, instinct supplied them, and Laura's instinct told her they were going to have a wonderful day the moment she saw Karl's car pull up outside the house just before nine the following morning. She waved down to him, having explained yesterday that it was pointless him coming up four floors.

The picnic hamper was already on the back seat of

the sleek, open-topped sports car, and as he came round
to open the door for her, she was surprised that he was
wearing a pair of minuscule white shorts! His long,
suntanned legs were tightly muscled; his short-sleeved
sports shirt displaying equally strong arms, covered
with a light down of little dark hairs ... She wondered
if he played squash—water-skied. There was so much to
find out about this man—so much he hadn't told her.
Was he married? Laura didn't want to think about that.
But as she climbed into the car she was smiling again;
hadn't her instinct told her this was going to be a
glorious day?

And she had been right. The magical day passed in a
pink haze. Andelys basked in the approaching midday
heat. They parked by the little marina, then strolled
through the quaint, narrow streets, Karl took her hand
as they slowly climbed the rough, dusty track up to the
castle, and then he stood beside her, a hand resting
lightly on her shoulder as they gazed down at the
splendid curve of the Seine bordered by cliffs and
smooth pastures. Barges crept up and down stream,
using a long island as a one-way traffic system. They
could see the little marina, the boats toy-tiny tucked
away from the busy stream. But it didn't seem busy
today, everything was hot and slow—except for a
butterfly which whizzed past her nose, and Karl
laughed ... Then she had to tell him what she knew
about the ruined castle, which wasn't much, except that
it had once been a stronghold of Richard Coeur de
Lion and was called Château Gaillard. And standing in
the shade of a crumbling wall, he looked about to kiss
her.

But he didn't. Instead, he picked her a little wild
flower, and the pink haze of a crazy day continued as
they strolled back down, bought a fresh *baguette* for
lunch and carried the picnic hamper carefully down the
steps and along the slatted catwalk where little dinghies
dozed in the midday heat. Some of them were very
small, but he led the way to a little day-boat with a tiny

cabin forward, and an inboard engine. It rocked as he helped her into it, and she sat down quickly. She wasn't quite sure if she liked boats.

There was hardly any breeze. The Seine was flat and heavy, mysterious—brilliant sunshine contrasted by dark, secret shadow. The little cruiser cut smoothly through the water; Laura relaxed, until a giant, articulated-type barge overtook them and sent a tidal wave of wash rolling towards the bank. Their boat rocked and she clutched at the gunwale until her knuckles showed white.

Karl cursed and headed into the wave, and she felt slightly better going up and down instead of rolling from side to side. 'We will go over to the island—yes?' he suggested, and with relief she found herself pulling them under the overhanging trees until they found a spot where they could climb ashore.

That was better.

They picnicked under the trees, sunlight dappling down on them as they drank wine, ate bread, cheese and pâté. There were peaches, grapes ... more wine. Then they sunbathed, Karl took off his shirt and Laura selfconsciously slipped out of her sundress, having already put on her bikini underneath. She was feeling very happy with the world, it was rather nice to be surrounded by water, alone—cut off. Her pulses began a slow and heavy throb ... Cut off with a man who looked ... She cast him a covert glance, who looked exactly as a man ought to look, who made her body react in a way it had never done before. *Could* you fall in love with someone because they put three teaspoons of sugar in their coffee? She rolled on her stomach, picked up her suntan cream, and in a most daring fashion, asked him if he would cream her back.

He hesitated. For a brief second he didn't make a move and her heart sank. Then his eyes melted and he took the tube. She lay down flat again, her heart pounding now, her eyes tight shut, forcing herself to relax.

It was exquisite torture. The ice-cold cream soon warmed under the pressure of his hands. He was firm, businesslike—almost rough ... Her shoulders first, then her waist and lower back. But then he undid her bra to cream the bit underneath the strap ... and slowly his hand gentled as his fingers traced a delicate line down her spine—and all the way up again. She shivered and heard a soft little moan escape his lips.

'Such temptation,' he murmured, 'such promise of pleasure,' and his words were the final intoxication she needed.

Slowly, innocently seductive, she rolled over. Her bikini top was left behind—completely forgotten—and fierce blue eyes gazed down at the smooth, curvaceous length of her—until finally he lowered his lips to hers.

The kiss was brief, a featherlight touch on her parted mouth. Then he kissed her chin, her closed eyes. Not really kisses, but tiny, tiny, sensual spots of fire. Now he was nibbling her ear, nuzzling into the sensitive curve of her neck ... and lower, kissing her shoulder, midriff, tummy. Then he raised his head and his eyes were dark with desire as they lingered over her white breasts.

'Karl,' she whispered softly, reaching up to touch where a muscle was jerking in his cheek. 'Kiss me,' she implored, curling a hand around his neck and drawing him inexorably nearer ... nearer ...

A tremor ran through him and she saw a dangerous light ignite in his eyes before his lips came down to claim her. This time the kiss was dynamite, his lips hungrily parting hers, drowning her in unknown emotion. She moved restlessly beneath him, responding with rising need and passion. Oh, this wasn't really happening, it was all a dream. She wasn't really lying under the trees, practically naked, with the most magnificent man she had ever seen, the only man she had ever wanted. Nothing remotely like this had ever happened before. His lips were a revelation ... she was drowning in love, waves of heat and desire flooding her body as his hand caressed and eased its way down the intimate curves of her body. She groaned again and clutched at his broad, bare shoulders.

'Oh, Karl—yes!'

'That's nice—like this . . .'

'Yes—oh God, yes. Please,' she broke off, groaning again, arching herself nearer . . . 'please don't stop.'

And he didn't seem to have any intention of stopping; his whole body was on fire for her, his lips remorseless on the burgeoning tip of her breast.

She took a deep, shaky breath and flattened her palms in long, hungry caresses down his back. His skin felt good, warm, smooth, vital, yet beneath she could feel muscles tightening in masculine aggression. She was driving him crazy—they were driving each other crazy.

Not far away a slow, steady work-boat gave two short blasts of its horn in some secret language of the river. It wasn't really an intrusion, they were safe and secret on their cool green island. But Karl groaned and reluctantly raised his head, his face taut and serious, the blue eyes searing her face, seeing innocence, excitement, passion—fear?

He rolled off her, twisting away, and reaching into the picnic basket he poured himself half a glass of wine.

Laura stared at his broad, naked back. What had happened? What had she done wrong? Surely he didn't think the boatman could see?

She scrabbled up, afternoon sunlight, dancing through the leaves, playing a patchwork of movement on her bare skin. She touched his shoulder and he put down the glass, spilling some of the wine on to the grass.

'We must go back.' His voice was gentle but firm. 'It's getting late, Laura—I have a business dinner . . .' But all the while his greedy eyes feasted on the slim curves of her young, inexperienced body. 'Come.' He reached for her sundress and allowed himself the exquisite agony of helping her back into it.

His touch was fire and she trembled as he tied the

shoulder straps into little bows. He was very dexterous
with women's clothing. How much practice had he had?
Which was a silly thing to think, because a man like
Karl Rievenbeck would be very experienced indeed. Her
lips tightened and she frowned in a confusion of
wanting him, of feeling hurt, betrayed, let down—
frustrated.

He raised her chin, and his magnetic, dangerous force
of will made her look into his eyes. 'Don't be cross with
me, *liebling*,' he said softly. 'Believe me—the time is not
yet right.'

Time? What time did they have? Tomorrow was
Thursday, he would be leaving Paris the day after.

And as if reading her mind, he smiled crookedly and
kissed her forehead. 'We have all the time in the world,'
he whispered into her hair. 'To rush would be
criminal—yes?' Irresistibly their bodies swayed together,
and there was a warmth, an instinctive blending, mutual
trust—sharing.

'I—suppose so,' she said, still unsure, and their lips
found each other's of their own volition . . . it was like
the sealing of a precious, life-long pact.

So it was still a rosy day as they piled everything back
on board the little boat and gently headed back
upstream to Les Andelys. Laura settled comfortably in
the little cockpit, sunglasses protecting her eyes from
the dazzling, sultry afternoon sun. The river wound in a
giant curve, it was timeless, majestical, fringed with
dark bowing trees . . . Laura half-closed her eyes and
saw only light and shade, shadow, movement, sunlight
refracted into a million hazy bursts of colour. It made a
picture worthy of Monet.

It was nearly seven o'clock when they finally pulled
up outside her flat, and Karl kissed her, a long,
sensuous, open-to-the-public's-gaze type of kiss, and he
laughed when she blushed, and whispered, 'Tomorrow?'
and when she nodded he said he would collect her
about eight.

She could still feel the lingering taste of his lips as

she ran light-heartedly up the stairs. We have all the time in the world, he had said, all the time in the world ... He did love her. He *had* to love her. Surely a man wouldn't say a thing like that—not make it sound permanent.

The flat was empty and she was glad of the privacy. She turned on the radio and sang away to a popular song. It was all a sunlit dream, it had been the most perfect day of her life, but as she strolled into the kitchen to put the kettle on, she saw the message on the blackboard and her heart stopped.

Anthea's in town, it told her, *phone right away*, and beneath it was the name of a smart hotel and a room number.

Anthea here in Paris! Why?

'Laura, where the hell have you been? I've been trying to reach you all day!' Anthea sounded in her usual form, on the other end of the line.

'I've been out. What's the matter! I've been trying to phone you at home.'

'You come over here and I'll tell you what's the matter.'

Laura sighed. 'Now?'

'It's too late now, we're going out soon. Make it tomorrow—five o'clock.' That was all. Anthea slammed down the phone, but she was far more volatile the following day.

'My God, you look awful! What possessed you to come in those dreadful jeans—they reek of turps!' Anthea Grant's advance on her stepdaughter was hastily checked. She was a tall, striking red-head, and although she looked, and was, forty, Laura doubted she would age in the next twenty years.

'I've come straight from the Louvre,' said Laura. 'I've been painting all day.'

'Yes, well, that will have to stop now.' Anthea Grant reached for a cigarette; they were in her private suite, Laura didn't realise they had money for that kind of extravagance.

'What do you mean, stop? Stop painting? That's impossible—I'm going to be an illustrator.'

'Be what you like,' Anthea interrupted. 'But there's not more art school. No more Paris. What I'm saying, Laura dear, is there's no more money.'

'I—don't understand.'

'I'm not surprised. A shock, isn't it?' Her stepmother inhaled deeply, then blew a thin spiral of smoke up above her head. She was wearing a cool linen dress, cream, simply cut and expensive . . . and there was this hotel suite . . . it didn't make sense. She saw Laura's train of thought and her red lips laughed cruelly. 'Don't think this has anything to do with me,' she said bitterly. 'I'm staying here with an old school friend; she's paying for it all. We're doing a tour of Europe. A very wealthy woman—have I ever told you about Rachel Burton?' Laura couldn't remember, not that it mattered anyway. 'We've kept in touch all these years,' Anthea continued, sinking gracefully into a settee and crossing her long elegant legs. 'She's divorced from a wealthy Greek. In shipping, he was—still is, I suppose. Either way, he keeps Rachel in this kind of comfort.' She got up restlessly and stubbed out the cigarette in a dainty blue and white china ashtray. But the red-tipped fingers were aggressive, brutal, bending the half smoked cigarette, doubling it over—annihilating it . . . 'And now it's my turn. Your father took me for a fool, Laura, but I don't get taken twice.'

'Don't you speak about Daddy like that!' Laura retorted.

'Oh, hoity-toity.' Anthea's dark eyes were venomous. 'Then it's about time you found out about your precious "Daddy dear". Very grand, wasn't he? A fine figure of a man. But did you know his engineering firm had been losing money for the past ten years?'

'No!' Laura's green eyes widened in disbelief.

'Yes!' Anthea retaliated. 'And the grand house in Surrey was mortgaged,' she waved a hand, 'up to here!'

'I don't believe you.'

Anthea shrugged. 'Why should you? I took a bit of convincing, believe me. Oh, he put on a fine show. Daughter privately educated—at art school in Paris. Expensive cars—expensive holidays.' Bitterness shaped the words. 'But I have more business sense in my little finger than he had in all of his fat, stupid head!'

'Stop it!' Laura marched up to her stepmother, glaring at her, standing only a few inches away. 'He had fast cars and expensive holidays because that's what you wanted. It wasn't like that before. And how many companies have crashed these past years through no fault of their own? It's been the economic recession.'

Anthea pushed her away and there was no sympathy in the hard, angular lines of her face. 'Well, now I'm going to have an economic recession of my own,' she said nastily. 'I've sold everything—the company, what was left of it; the house; both cars . . .'

'You can't!' Laura was practically speechless.

'Yes, I can.' Savage eyes flashed with triumph. 'It's all gone—the lot. Much good any of it would have done us. And between it all I've managed to buy a flat.'

'Where?' Surely her home, the place where she had grown up—surely it hadn't simply disappeared without anything being said? What about her favourite bits of furniture? And—oh no, what about those pictures her mother had painted? . . .

Anthea was shuddering. 'It's in some appalling little backwater in Islington,' she said. 'There's a room for you, so there's no need to say I haven't done my duty. I read the will, you know. Every line. It all came to me so long as I provided you with a home. Hah! Some home! Some inheritance!'

'But what about all my things?' asked Laura, already quite pale.

'*My* things,' Anthea corrected. 'I sold the antiques I didn't need for the flat, the rest of the stuff went for jumble—a man came and cleared the lot. I had a firm offer soon after I put the house on the market. But they wanted a quick completion. Surely you're not bothered about a few old bits and pieces?'

'But the paintings?' Laura almost sobbed.

'Some dealer came. There was nothing of any value. He gave me eighty pounds for the lot.'

Laura stood for a moment in shocked silence. Gone—the last fragile link with the mother she had never known. No, they wouldn't be worth anything. They had been the immature beginning of a fresh new art ... she turned away, her eyes filling with tears, but determined that Anthea shouldn't see. 'I'm not coming back to London,' she managed to say firmly. 'I've made friends here. If I can't afford to go to art school, I'll get myself a job. My French is pretty good really.'

'Quite frankly, Laura, I don't give a damn where you go. *If* you go back to London, you'll have to share the flat with Vincent for a while. Remember him, do you? From when you came home last Easter? He's a sweetie—but absolutely broke. Mind you,' her eyes flickered up and down Laura in growing pity and contempt, 'you're not his usual type, but as I won't be around for the summer, he might do you a bit of good. Time you grew up, Laura, time you realised this is a tough old world and all a woman can do is fight.'

It took all Laura's determination not to respond to such a low, vile attack. Instead she took a steadying breath and said, 'What about all my things? Clothes, books, sketches.'

Anthea turned away, uninterested. 'Vincent shifted a great pile of junk in your room and took it up to the flat. I told you he's a sweetie. Perhaps if you tidied yourself up a bit ...'

'Look, I told you—I've been painting all day.'

'Yes, well, run along back there, or wherever you're going. I need a rest before going out this evening. Rachel will be up from the salon in a minute and she won't want the place smelling of an artist's studio.'

'Right. Don't worry, I'm going.' Now the time had

come, Laura felt suddenly bereft. Anthea was all she had.

Her stepmother picked up a magazine and settled herself in a chair by the opened window. The long net curtains billowed in the breeze as the afternoon sun slanted sideways into the elegant room. It looked all so peaceful ... 'By the way,' she said, when Laura had reached the door and was somehow reluctant to leave, 'we shall be here over the weekend—let me know what you decide to do. *If* you go back to London, I'll have to warn poor Vincent.'

Laura walked back to the flat in a daze. She had lost everything now, father, home—all the intimate, un-important but special things that make up a life. And worst of all was the loss of the paintings that had been a special link with her mother. And they had become more special over the years as it had become clear Laura was continuing her mother's talent.

The flat was full of people, all the girls and one or two friends, it was so *crowded*. For the first time Laura felt she needed space and peace. The bathroom was still a mess, but she showered and washed her hair, her movements slow and automatic, trying to feel enthusi-astic about tonight—but it was Karl's last night and she felt sad already about that as well.

The phone rang; it was Karl to say he had been delayed in a meeting and was it all right if he sent a car over for her at eight?

She smiled wearily. 'Of course.'

'Are you all right, Laura?'

'Fine. The—er—flat's full of people.' So he took her sadness for shyness, and really what did it *matter*? This was only a game to him—he was only whiling away a few lonely hours away from home.

A great corkscrew of tension was twisting itself inside her, but somehow she managed to dress and fix her face, and at five minutes to eight she stared at her reflection in the wardrobe mirror and had to admit, 'Not bad.' The cool, scanty slip of a dress showed off her suntan and exactly matched her eyes. And then she realised that she didn't want the chauffeur coming all the way up here and ringing the bell, she didn't want the girls to think ... Think what? That she had found some rich sugar-daddy? That she was showing off? So she grabbed her bag and raced downstairs, and luckily met the chauffeur on the way up. He was short and rather round, and she was glad he hadn't had to struggle any further.

The car obviously belonged to the firm Karl worked for. It wasn't a car, it was a limousine, and she sat back in overpowering comfort as it cruised through deserted side streets, heaven alone knew where they were going, perhaps she ought to keep a lookout. Once they crossed a busy intersection, but Laura was soon lost in a maze of heavy stone buildings. They passed banks, embassies, one or two select antique shops and private art galleries. Eventually they pulled up in a narrow side street, the low evening sun trapped behind the imposing building they were about to enter. It wasn't the main door; there was no name and no windows visible on the ground floor. The chauffeur unlocked an anonymous carved door and ushered her quickly into a little panelled hallway, where the only door out of it was obviously a lift.

'Monsieur Rievenbeck is above,' he said in English, and Laura found herself whisked upwards in swift silence. What on earth was this place?

As the door swished open Karl was waiting for her, his hair damp as if he had just rushed from the shower. And she had the feeling that he had been hastily tucking in his shirt.

'Laura, my love, I am sorry about this.' He took her hand and kissed it; not flamboyantly, but as a tender, natural gesture. Laura held her breath. No one had ever kissed her hand before! 'I've spent all day in Rouen— these meetings go on and on. Come—have a drink,' and he led her from the elegant reception area where there had been a little table with a bowl of roses, into the stunning vision of cool green and white which, for want

of a better name, one could call a living room. It was on
two levels, off-white carpet covered the huge living area,
then climbed two shallow steps to the circular glass
dining table and bamboo chairs. There were splashes of
vivid green from pot plants, contrasted by white leather
settees, and a glass and chrome coffee table. She liked the
large elegant table lamps on onyx stands. Elegant but
masculine, with a copy of a brightly coloured Mondrian
hanging over the fireplace. But better even than that
were the floor-to-ceiling glass doors which had been
opened now as the heat of the day had abated. Karl led
her outside to a roof garden, with real grass and a
fountain—and the most superb bird's eye view of Paris.

'I don't believe it—it's beautiful!' she smiled, and he
seemed pleased and also a little surprised at her
enthusiasm. 'Is it a company flat?' she asked, when he
returned with her drink, and he nodded in an offhand
way that showed he didn't want to talk about anything
as boring as that.

'I thought we would go out to dinner somewhere
special,' he said, coming to join her as she stared down
at the tumbled rooftops and the distant curve of the
river. She could see the Eiffel Tower from here, misty
with the heat and fumes of a day's heavy traffic. 'I've
missed you,' he whispered, touching her bare arm with
the lightest of fingers and letting his thumb tease the
sensitive spot inside her elbow. 'I kept wishing it was
yesterday . . .' His breath was warm in her hair—in her
ear. 'I didn't want to be in an airless boardroom—I
wanted to be with you.'

Laura closed her eyes and leant back against the
hard, familiar, exciting length of him. She held her
breath as he nibbled her ear, kissed the curve of her
neck, her nape, then followed the delicate column of
her spine.

'Beautiful,' he murmured, 'beautiful,' and then he
was taking her glass, putting it down on the parapet,
and turning her round to face him. 'You feel it too,
don't you, Laura? Tell me it isn't imagination.'

His kiss was liquid fire, their bodies blending together as if they had been lovers for all time. Her hands smoothed between the open fronts of his shirt—it was a very nice dress shirt with tiny, tiny pleats down the front. He smelt good, oh, how good; clean, fresh, masculine, potent—and how, *how* was she going to live after he went away tomorrow? Emotion welled up inside her—she tried to swallow it down, but it wouldn't go.

'Laura, *liebling*,' he was holding her head in his hands, strong thumbs stroking her cheeks as the first tears fell. 'What's wrong? Why are you upset?'

She broke away from him, cross with herself for appearing like a naïve child when he was obviously used to women as experienced as himself. 'You speak far too much German for an Italian,' she chided, trying to lighten the atmosphere as she searched in her little patchwork bag for a hanky.

'Do I?' His smile tempted one of her own. 'We speak both at home . . .' he broke off, his eyes searching her face. 'But you are really upset,' and he gathered her against him and her shoulders shook in a silent sob. 'Tell me.'

'I can't.'

'Yes, you can.' He led her to a swinging seat under a colourful canopy and they sat rocking gently, he with an arm round her, she snuggling against the firm protection of his chest.

She told him all about it; about the house being sold, about art college having to finish . . . and in a tiny voice she told him about her mother's paintings that she would never see again. As she did so his hand smoothed her hair and his breathing was deep and slow, deep and slow, as if he was forcing calmness upon himself. He let her cry for as long as she wanted, but she couldn't tell him that half her tears were shed for him . . . because after tomorrow she would be so *alone*.

The bells from three nearby churches chimed nine o'clock—quarter past—half past. At last there was peace, the long daylight shadows of a summer evening gradually mellowing, softening ... The little fountain bubbled and danced in a soothing rhythm of its own. Laura wanted this moment to go on for ever. But at last Karl was stirring beside her and she sat up and patted her blonde curls, not knowing quite what to say.

'Do you still wish to go out?' he said, brushing a light finger across her cheek.

Lord, his dinner—he must be ravenous! But she couldn't face a smart restaurant where she would have to be lighthearted and share him with all those other people. 'I'd rather stay here,' she said, looking down at her crumpled hanky.

His fingers slid under her chin, tilting her face up; green, troubled eyes mirrored her pain. His face hardened, softened. 'That may not be very wise, little one.'

Suddenly Laura didn't want to be very wise. 'I couldn't face all those people,' she coaxed, without knowing what the inflection in her voice was doing to him.

A muscle jerked in his cheek and she lifted her hand up to still it. He smiled, oh, such a serious smile, before whispering, 'I'll go and cancel the table.'

CHAPTER THREE

THERE were lights down in the soft grey city now. Laura strolled over to the parapet, hearing Karl's superb French as he talked on the telephone. He really was a very accomplished, very complex man. He must hold an important position if he had the use of this flat. She still didn't know who he worked for; presumably the company downstairs. He had finished on the phone now, and she heard him switching on the table lamps; it darkened the terrace a little.

'Could you eat something now?' he asked, stepping back outside and strolling over to play gently with her fingers. 'Something light, perhaps? An omelette?'

She nodded. But she couldn't sit down outside and relax—away from him, when it was getting on for ten o'clock—only two short hours to Friday . . .

So they prepared supper together. Just from bits and pieces in the fridge, they filled the dining table with salad, cheeses, pâté, fruit, cheesecake . . . and Karl's thick, frothy omelettes seasoned with fresh herbs. There was a bottle of wine, and the meal was eaten with the poignant sweetness of the gentle sound of a Schubert symphony.

'Is it essential that you go to art college?' Karl asked, slicing a peach and passing half across to her.

'Not to get a job,' she said, 'but to develop my talent—definitely yes.' And because she didn't want him to feel sorry for her, she added, 'But I can do it part time—it will take longer, that's all.'

He thoughtfully sliced his half of the peach into segments. 'Is it necessary for you to remain in Paris? Is there here perhaps a special teacher?'

Laura smiled at him, her soft, suntanned skin eminently touchable in the light from the table lamp.

'Paris is a luxury—I could just as well learn in London.'

'But you have no wish to return to your stepmother's flat?'

'Oh, no.'

There was an awkward little silence. The tape finished and clicked itself off. Karl suggested they take their coffee out on to the terrace, and this time he only put one spoonful of sugar in his cup. How strange!

Outside, it was dark at last, really middle-of-the-night black which would last only a few short hours at this time of the year. A thick trace of city lights spread like a glittering carpet below, and they stood and drank their coffee in silence, watching it. Then they went and sat together in the double swinging seat, arms and thighs lightly touching ... He played gently with her fingers, raising them to his lips now and then.

Laura closed her eyes and ached inside. She wanted him to kiss her properly. She desperately needed to be loved. They had such a few short hours left together. Karl hadn't said anything about seeing her again. In fact, he seemed to be disappearing into himself. Was he regretting that he had brought her here? Was he deciding he didn't want to get involved? Back and forth, back and forth, gently the swing rocked in time with the throb of life pulsing deep inside her. Clocks began chiming midnight and Laura held her breath.

It was Friday.

'You've had a distressing day,' Karl began quietly. 'You must be tired.' His thumb stroked her palm. 'I ought to take you home.'

She made no reply, but instead turned her head and gazed up at him with wide, imploring eyes.

'Laura, *liebling*,' his fractured accent shook, 'don't look at me like that—I'm trying ... ' yet his hand came up and caressed her cheek.

'I don't want to go,' she whispered.

'I don't want you to go either.' His eyes were all over

her, on her face, her neck, lingering on the swell of
green chiffon that covered her breasts.

'Well, then?' she said, knowing in a moment he
would kiss her properly. Without realising, she
moistened her full lower lip.

'But we need to talk. We haven't discussed things.
You don't know anything about me.'

'Are you married?' she asked in a tiny voice, because
he had given her the opening.

The question seemed both to amuse and astound
him. 'No, Laura—no, I'm not married. Remarkable,
isn't it?'

Yes. She couldn't imagine why someone hadn't
snapped him up years ago. Suddenly her heart began to
sing.

'But——' He didn't seem convinced that his last
remark had made everything all right. 'Look at you,' he
continued. 'How old are you? Twenty-one? Twenty-
two?'

'Nineteen,' she whispered, glancing at him quickly
and seeing him close his eyes in horror. 'But I shall be
twenty in a few weeks' time.'

'Ah.' He opened his eyes again, a little smile hovering
around his lips. 'And that makes all the difference,
doesn't it?' He was laughing at her and she felt silly and
confused. The clocks started striking the quarter hour—
they were slightly out of synchronisation. She wanted
all the clocks in the world to stop. She wanted to stay
up on this roof garden with Karl for ever. He bent his
head and kissed her, his lips lightly brushing her own
before gently chewing her bottom lip. 'I'm thirty-five,'
he murmured against her cheek. 'Fifteen years . . .' now
he was nibbling her ear, 'is a lot.'

'Are you saying I'm too young for you?'

He shook his head. 'I'm too old for you.'

She ran her hand down his chest, the shirt was
smooth silk and she felt his heart hammering in time
with her own. It was a shock to realise he was so
emotionally affected. It gave her courage to say,

seductively, 'Perhaps I'm the one to judge if you're too old for me, and I don't think you are at all ...'

'Don't you?' He captured her hand and raised it to his lips. His eyes laughing, serious, thoughtful. 'Don't you really?' and then he was gathering her into his arms and groaning softly as their bodies nestled in secret, intimate corners. 'I've wanted you so much, Laura— and now, now, *Ich werde dich nie gehen lassen*,' only she couldn't understand when he spoke in German. Then he eased her from him, sighing deeply, looking down at her with a new sort of specialness. 'You wish—to stay tonight?' he asked, stroking her hair, and it was all soft and warm with an instinctive blending.

'Yes, please,' she whispered into his shoulder.

His eyes were dark and serious. 'You know what will happen if you stay?'

She nodded.

'You are sure?'

She nodded again.

'Tell me.'

'Yes, Karl, I'm sure.' And because she simply had to convince him, she added, 'I want to spend the night with you. I want you to make love to me.'

The dark, warm, silent summer night was all around them. It enveloped their senses, suspending time, thought, rationality. Judgments, morals, were left behind in the glittering sunlight of day. Up here in the dark world love danced between them like the entwining moths above their heads.

'Come, then.' He held her lightly, brushing their bodies tantalisingly together. 'We have wanted this from the beginning—all the rest can wait ...' And he swung her into his arms and carried her through to the bedroom.

Laura knew a moment's panic when she saw the giant king-size bed, draped in regal royal blue. There was white carpet in here as well, and walls of fitted cupboards; the dressing table was masculine and bare. The room was dimly lit by one table lamp next to the bed, and it softened the otherwise harsh lines of the room to an almost palpable seductivity.

He let her feet slide to the floor, she had taken her sandals off ages ago, and now her bare feet sank into the thick pile. He kissed her, a multitude of tiny, tiny kisses covering her face, her throat, mingling with her hair . . . finding their way into her ear.

She shivered and he smiled, slowly sliding the thin straps off her shoulders, and she threw her head back, revelling in his touch as his lips travelled dangerously towards her cleavage. His hands slid down her arms, down her back and firmed against her bottom, drawing her nearer. Excitement and a piercing heat inflamed her body as it made magnetic contact with him.

'You're sure?' he whispered again, and she nodded and clung on to him, her fingers biting into his arms despite their covering of silk. 'Have you . . . before?' he asked, and when she shook her head, he groaned in satisfaction, and added, 'I thought not,' while her zip began sliding undone.

Laura held her breath, amazed that she wasn't paralysed with shame. Knowing exactly what she was doing—yet stunned at herself for doing it. What had happened to her policy of keeping the men in her life at arm's length? Maybe she had only been waiting for the right man. And Karl *was* the right man—she knew that instinctively.

At last the dress was undone and he let it fall to her waist, her brief lacy bra a taunting challenge to nakedness, and his eyes were dark, smouldering—greedy. He kissed the gentle valley between her breasts, his hair smooth and soft against her body, and she closed her eyes, willing him to kiss her like this for ever.

His hands began moving over her body again, her dress completely unzipped now, and he let it fall limply around her ankles, her lacy bikini pants a provocation rather than protection. He liked them, in fact she could tell he liked everything as he smoothed her thighs, hips, stomach . . .

Then he seemed to sense her sudden nerves, and he eased her from him, capturing her hands and taking them up to his chest. 'Now it's your turn,' he said, smiling wickedly, and her fingers trembled as she struggled with the unfamiliar back-to-front buttons, and she knew she wasn't being as slow and sexy as he had been.

In the end he helped her, and when he reached for the buckle of his belt, she turned away and felt warmth rush to her cheeks. She was crazy—this whole situation was dynamite. She couldn't cope with an experienced man like Karl, who undressed in front of a woman without reserve. And for a moment she wondered how many times he had done this kind of thing before—and with what kind of women?

Lost in her thoughts, she didn't hear him cross the carpet to her side, and as he turned her round in his arms she realised he was completely naked.

Lord, how magnificent he was! She closed her eyes almost believing she would faint, but the smooth hardness of his body both frightened yet excited her. She tentatively brushed against his chest, almost hypnotised by the virile smattering of dark chest hairs plunging in a deep line down below his waist. He felt good, oh, how good, and now he was drawing her closer, sharing the intimacy of his arousal, and she gasped as her body demonstrated her need of him; her need, her craving—and her undying love.

'Laura.' His eyes held her so that she couldn't move, not that she wanted to . . . The bra came off . . . slowly, sensuously, making her shiver with delight. 'Beautiful,' he murmured, bending his head to kiss the burgeoning tip of each breast.

It was exquisite agony; his hands warm, firm, coaxing; his lips gentle, taunting, driving her wild. Then his hands were sliding lower, and he knelt in front of her, delicately manoeuvring her lacy bikini pants over her thighs.

'Karl!' she gasped on a tiny breath, because this

couldn't possibly be happening, she wasn't really
standing here, being undressed and, oh, kissed like this
... his lips and tongue awakening the full blooming of
her womanhood. Childish fantasies were left behind for
ever; with intimate tenderness he completed her arousal
so that she finally clutched at his shoulders and begged
him to make love to her.

'Hush,' he whispered, his face strained in the effort of
controlling his emotions. 'Laura, you feel it is right—
yes?' he breathed, and at last she was in his arms and he
was carrying her across to the bed.

'I—want you so badly.' She was almost crying,
overwhelmed with love—overwhelmed by love. 'Please,
Karl—please!' and he groaned softly as she reached for
him, her green eyes wide and imploring.

He lay down beside her in the great bed, the duvet
pushed out of the way, their eyes devouring each
other's body, and Laura caressed his hip, kissed his
chest, then lower, to the flat, hard stomach. He liked
it, oh yes, he liked it, moving restlessly—his hand
searching for one of hers. So she kissed him again,
amazed at the way she was handling the situation,
amazed that she wasn't shrinking into the pillows
—scared and bashful. Courage made her push him
back into the pillows, her body gliding over him in a
naked, lingering caress.

It was too much for him. His eyes flashed
dangerously and sudden alarm leapt in her stomach as
he rolled over, trapping her, pinning her helplessly.
Now his kiss was firm and demanding, parting her lips
to plunder the dark warmth of her mouth. His body
moved nearer in an embrace of inevitability, and Laura
groaned and lifted herself towards him ... But the
violence of his kiss had ended, he was very, very still,
blue eyes wary, concerned—shining with desire.

'Laura, my love—you are sure?'

'Don't keep saying that,' she breathed frantically.

'But I think I might hurt you.'

She screwed up her eyes. 'It doesn't *matter*.' And

she reached for him hungrily—demanding his possession. It was the final assurance he needed.

'Did I hurt you?' Karl whispered, how many hours
afterwards, Laura simply couldn't have said.

She smiled, slow and fat—like a cat. 'I don't
remember.'

His tongue flicked erotically around her ear. 'Don't
you remember anything?'

She giggled. 'Silly!' The sun shone full on them as
they snuggled together, their bare legs entwined, already
familiar with each other.

He kissed her and, as easily as that, it all started
again. He saw the look in her eyes and broke away.
'Forgive me, darling, we should have woken earlier—
but it's after eight o'clock, and I have a very important
meeting.' And there was something in his eyes, some
strange preoccupation that made her go a little cold
inside. 'You stay there—rest,' and although his kiss
lingered for a while, he somehow dragged himself out of
bed and padded over to the bathroom.

Laura snuggled down on his side of the bed,
savouring his warmth, the smell of aftershave on the
bed cover which mingled with the intimate musky tang
of the male. What was the matter? Why had he left her
so suddenly? What would happen now?

It was Friday! Remembering made her suddenly feel
sick. What time would he leave Paris? *Please* let him
want to see her again! But she mustn't appear naïve.
She mustn't become tearful and clingy—that would be
dreadful. So she struggled up and tottered over to their
heap of last night's clothes. She wore his shirt; it came
down to her knees and she had to roll up the sleeves
until her hands appeared.

She prepared breakfast. Karl was pleased, but still
preoccupied. They had orange juice, toast, coffee,
scrambled eggs. He said she was adorable and a superb
cook . . . but that was all.

She stared at him across the table in the spotless pine

kitchen. He was being briskly efficient, reading his mail
and sifting through some important-looking papers in
his slim briefcase. Was he trying to tell her something?
Laura finally understood.

'Look,' she began, having difficulty swallowing her
final piece of toast, 'about last night.' Good, she had his
attention. Lord, how handsome he was in his dark
business suit and pale blue shirt that exactly matched
the colour of his eyes. 'I—know I haven't done this
kind of thing before,' she stumbled on. 'But—well, this
is the twentieth century—and I'm quite grown-up, you
know ...'

He replaced his coffee cup in the saucer, his eyes
quietly thoughtful, never leaving her face.

'What are you trying to tell me, Laura?' His quiet,
fractured accent had an edge to it—an edge she couldn't
quite name.

'I—don't want you to think—because of what
happened—that I expect ...'

'That you expect me to propose marriage,' he
finished for her. His eyes were still grave, but the
corners of his mouth had momentarily lifted.

'Yes. You see, there's no need. Not these days ...'
She broke off as he put down a crisp white document
and possessed himself of both her hands.

'But there is every need,' he said. 'Not because of
what happened last night—but because I *want* to marry
you. Ever since last week. You are far more beautiful
than the Mona Lisa. You do love me—don't you?' he
continued urgently, and Laura could only gulp and nod
and somehow her eyes were full of tears. He came
round the table and gathered her up in his arms. 'Does
the prospect of marrying me make you feel that bad?'

'Silly!'

'Then smile for me.' He lifted her chin, but she didn't
have time to smile because he was groaning and kissing
her again, and they were lost in the consuming passion
of love ...

'Enough,' he said eventually, breaking the kiss and

putting her purposefully from him. 'You must get dressed. The car will be here in twenty minutes and I'll drop you home on the way to my meeting.'

'Is it Rouen again?'

'Yes.'

So she showered and dressed in ten minutes flat. She had been told not to touch the dishes because they would be 'done'. What luxury! In the end she was ready before Karl, and she wandered around the living room, looking out towards the river which was still obscured in the early morning haze. It would be hot again today. Then the painting caught her eye, she really did like Mondrian in a crazy sort of way. It really was a very good copy . . . And then as she drew nearer she realised it was an original! No! But it was. And Karl came into the room, pleased at her interest.

'It's an original!' Her green eyes were wide with wonder.

He grinned—yet was somehow wary. 'One of my little weaknesses.'

'But it must be worth . . .?'

'I suppose so.' He was still quietly serious, thoughtful, watching her.

She took a deep breath. 'Just—who do you work for? What kind of company can afford wall decorations like this? What exactly is this place? Who *are* you, Karl?'

'I'm—a banker.'

'Oh—you mean you make money. Print it.' She glanced at the painting. 'That would explain.'

They laughed together.

'It isn't quite like that,' he said, serious again.

She sighed. 'No, I don't suppose it is.'

'I work very hard.'

'Yes.'

'So hard that I have to leave Paris this afternoon, and there's no way I can get out of it, darling.'

She peered up at him through her lashes. 'I realise that.'

'I have to be in Brussels.' He reached in his jacket

pocket and brought out a note pad. 'This will be my
phone number. Then London,' he scribbled another
number in bold, distinctive numerals. 'And then Rome,
I think.' He seemed only now to make the decision
about Rome. 'But you already have that number.'

Laura remembered the business card he had given
her, and nodded.

'Good.' But she must still have looked a little
woebegone, because he came across and took her lightly
in his arms, his fingers smoothing through her curls.
'Last night was wonderful,' he whispered, so that not
even the painting could hear, and only now did she
realise just how much she had needed that reassurance.
'It was perfect—I adore you—and I wish we could
spend the rest of the day in bed.'

Laura nestled into the blue silk shirt and smiled
contentedly. 'So do I,' she whispered back, and then, oh
dear, it was beginning again, the warmth and movement
as their bodies responded and aroused each other.

'Not now—it isn't possible,' he said, putting her
firmly from him and taking a long, steadying breath.
'I'll be away at least a week—maybe ten days.' It
seemed a lifetime to Laura. 'But I'll phone every day—
and then we'll be together . . .' And then he suddenly
seemed to remember something as he took his wallet
out of his pocket. 'I'll leave you some money.'

'No!' She took a step backwards, appalled at the
idea.

'But you said Anthea had stopped your allowance.
You'll need money, darling.'

'No—no. I'm all right—fine. *Really*,' she added
firmly, trying not to sound quite so hysterical. 'I've got
some savings, and my rent is paid up for several weeks.'

Karl decided not to press the point, which was just as
well, because the doorbell rang. The car had arrived to
take him to Rouen, and he kissed her quickly,
squeezing her hand and murmuring something soft and
tender in German. Laura wished he wouldn't keep
doing that!

She felt selfconscious wearing her evening dress at nine o'clock in the morning, especially as it was the same driver who had brought her here last night. But his face was inscrutable as they stepped out of the lift down in the ground floor vestibule.

'I would like to present the future Madame Rievenbeck,' Karl said in French, and while Laura's hand was shaken and they were congratulated, he continued smiling down at her; tall, bemused, proud— just like a dog with two tails. And Laura's burst of love was almost painful. At that very moment she felt as close to him as she had done during those incredible hours in bed.

She couldn't wait to tell the whole world, either!

'Married? *You?*' Anthea Grant laughed in spiteful disbelief, an unlit cigarette transfixed between her fingers in mid-air. 'This is all rather sudden, isn't it, my dear Laura?'

'I suppose so.' It had taken two days to pluck up the courage to come back to the hotel, two days for a miracle to turn into a dream—and what place did dreams have in reality? Did Karl *really* want to marry her? Laura wasn't surprised at Anthea's stunned amazement. Wait until she heard the rest!

'How long have you known him?' She was lighting her cigarette now, schooling her features into mild indifference.

'Not long,' said Laura.

'Thinks he's on to a good thing, does he?'

Laura's face froze. 'What's that supposed to mean?'

'Thinks he's found himself an heiress, does he?' her stepmother sneered. 'Daddy sending her to art school in Paris for a bit of fun . . .?'

'Do I *look* like an heiress?' Laura had been painting at the Louvre all day again and was still in her jeans.

Anthea inhaled deeply, then sank into a chair. There was no sign of her old school friend, thank heavens. Laura suggested that they phone down for some tea.

Anthea agreed, and they waited until it came in an unnatural silence.

'I thought you'd be pleased,' Laura continued, pouring two cups and passing her stepmother a plate of biscuits. Anthea shook her head. 'I mean—it does mean I'm off your hands,' she continued.

'You're off my hands whether you marry or not. I thought I made that quite clear the other day.'

'Perfectly,' Laura acknowledged tightly.

'Good. But that doesn't mean I'm going to let you marry someone totally unsuitable. Who is this fellow? What's his name? What does he do? Where does he come from?'

'He's Italian,' Laura began.

'Oh, my God, not some little Italian waiter—the world seems full of them!'

'He isn't a waiter—not that it would make any difference if he was,' yet that sounded naïve even to her own ears. She suspected that Karl's attraction lay not in his position or wealth, exactly, but in that self-assured directness, that dominant male ego that had made him succeed. 'He's—a business man,' she went on quickly, 'and his name's Karl.'

Anthea's eyes were shrewd and brittle, almost as if she was assessing this new situation from her own point of view. 'Karl who?' Her voice was tinged with sarcasm.

Laura found herself crossing her fingers behind her back. Why? 'Karl Rievenbeck,' she said, and Anthea's expression froze into incredulity.

'*Rievenbeck?* You mean *the* Rievenbecks?'

Laura swallowed. 'I don't know.'

'What d'you mean, you don't *know*?' Anthea snorted, getting up and pacing over to the window and back again. Her face was hostile, alive, spiteful—reluctantly amazed. 'If you're going to marry him, surely you know?'

'I know he's a banker . . .' Laura tried.

'I don't believe it,' her stepmother interrupted, still patrolling the small private sitting-room. 'Here am I searching Europe for a first-class meal ticket, and one lands straight in your lap. Don't tell me you haven't heard of Rievenbeck's, Vienna. They're only one of the most powerful merchant banks in Europe. Rachel—my friend here—was only talking about them the other day. She's got shares in a shipping company in Rouen who want to build a large new dock, or something. It's a multi-million-pound project—and they've approached Rievenbeck's for finance. It was in the papers. *Surely* you must have seen it—there was a picture . . .'

'I didn't know,' Laura stammered. 'I don't often read the papers. Karl,' she swallowed, 'Karl was in Rouen last week.'

Anthea began to laugh hysterically. 'It's a joke,' she said. 'It's some confidence trickster giving you a line— thinking you've got money—or trying to get you into his bed.' But that sounded ludicrous even to her. 'Where is he?' she asked, snapping out of herself and becoming hard and businesslike again. 'I want to see this Karl Rievenbeck. I want him to know he doesn't marry my stepdaughter as easily as that. There are certain conditions!' She was obviously thinking of some kind of cash payment—Laura couldn't believe it.

'I am over eighteen, you know. I don't need your consent.'

'There could be other considerations,' Anthea retorted. 'I could say some very unpleasant things about your father—about being broke—about caring for you, spending every penny I had, and then you up and leave me . . . I don't think the Rievenbecks would like that sort of scandal.'

'You wouldn't dare!' Laura breathed.

'Worried already?' Anthea laughed. 'Frightened you'll lose your grip on him?' She went back to the table where she had left her cigarette burning in the ashtray. 'Okay, maybe you're right,' she said, turning back to Laura, drawing deeply on her cigarette with an almost sensual enjoyment. 'Maybe I'll wait until you're safely married,' and before Laura could retaliate, she said, 'But I'll only give you a year—two at the most. You're a fool if you think a chit of a girl like you can keep a man like that happy.' Her mouth twisted nastily and as she marched over to the tea trolley her silk two-piece swished in mutual irritation. 'But lord knows why he wants to marry you,' she continued, pouring herself some more tea and complaining that it was now too strong. 'Are you pregnant? Not that that would make any difference—he could easily arrange . . .'

'No, I'm not pregnant!' Laura practically screamed. But supposing she was! Supposing . . .

Anthea didn't look surprised, she had always made it clear that she considered Laura gauche and unattractive. 'How old is this Karl Rievenbeck?' she asked suddenly. 'Getting on a bit, is he? Got a thing about little girls?' And that was too much for Laura, who picked up her raffia basket and stormed out.

She walked all the way back to the flat; furious with Anthea one moment, confused and in a crazy nightmare the next. Of course, it might not all be true, she thought, eventually letting herself into the flat. It might not be the same person. Where was the phone book? She found it under the settee and flipped through to the R's . . . There it was, Rievenbeck's, Vienna. It was spelt the same, and although she hadn't seen the name of the street when she had visited the flat, she knew it was the same area.

She took a steadying sigh and flopped down on to a floor cushion. So he really was *the* Karl Rievenbeck! And although she knew most girls would have been delighted, a nagging doubt dragged at her heart. It was all hopeless, of course, because if he was . . . she couldn't even *think* 'millionaire', so she settled for *wealthy*, then what was he doing bothering with her?

Unless he wants to marry me for some other reason. The thought leapt into her mind like a demon, because there was something powerful and dangerous about Karl; dangerous because it was cloaked in urbane sophistication. And when they had been in bed together, she had sensed the latent, dominant aggression of a proud, but very private, man. How was it possible to love someone, to want to marry them—yet be bewildered by them? Almost frightened! Was that her instinct working again, or simply pre-nuptial nerves?

CHAPTER FOUR

KARL was away nearly two weeks. The long hot spell had broken and there were ten days of dull, overcast weather, punctuated by rain and heavy thunderstorms. Laura's copy of *The Forge* wasn't coming on as well, or as quickly, as she had hoped. Perhaps because she had begun to try and find herself a job. It was a time-consuming occupation, carting her portfolio of sketches around to all the publishers, trying to get commissions. When she had tried all the publishers, she would begin on the advertising agencies ... She hadn't told any of her friends, because they would think she was mad; married to Karl she would hardly need to work for a living—and especially not in Paris. But supposing all that didn't work out? Supposing it had only been a dream?

But alone at nights, in her familiar narrow bed under the eaves, Laura had no difficulty in remembering the actuality of every moment of their short time together. Then, it wasn't the international banker and the little Miss Nobody, but a man and a woman, meeting—falling in love; touching, kissing, making love ...

Now she closed her eyes tightly and rolled over into the pillow. One night, that was all she had to remember, one long special night ... Her body awakened at the memory ... one night of Karl's shattering possession. She remembered the pain—and crying out—and then the unbelievable, the unimagined sweetness. And she wanted him here again—now. She wanted to hold him tightly against her. She wanted to feel the weight of him remorselessly pressing her into the bed. She wanted to feel the masculine magnificence of his body possessing her; his potent virility held back with a force of strength that had delighted yet amazed her. How tender he had been that very first time—how lethally passionate the next! She could feel him, smell him, *taste* him ... and he mingled with her restless dreams, tempting, tormenting—always just out of arm's reach. So that when day came she woke up unrefreshed and frustrated.

He phoned most days. First from Brussels, then from London, and the second weekend after he had left, he phoned from Rome. It was much later than his other calls had been—nearly midnight. Laura could hear soft music in the background; she had the feeling he wasn't phoning from a hotel.

'You were not in bed?' he asked quietly.

'No.' She couldn't add that she wouldn't have been able to go to sleep until he had phoned. 'How are you?'

'Missing you.' His voice was low, sexy, fractured. Then someone spoke to him and his reply was a long, fluid sentence in Italian.

'Are you staying with friends?' she asked, trying not to sound as if she was prying: that voice had sounded definitely female!

'I'm dining with friends.' His voice was cool, formal. 'I did not notice the time—I had intended phoning you back at the apartment.'

Did that mean that he wasn't going back to his flat tonight?

'Are you still there, Laura?'

'Yes.'

'Is anything the matter?'

'I'm—tired, that's all.'

And then he seemed cross with himself, and explained that he had to go on to Vienna tomorrow, and wouldn't be able to get back to Paris until Tuesday evening. That long? But then his voice lowered in intimate invitation, and he murmured, 'Will you come and cook my supper?'

Laura's palms went damp and a dull throb beat its familiar rhythm through her veins.

Tuesday. That was ages away. They said goodnight, and Laura curled up on the settee, excited, yet feeling a strange churning in her stomach. Why hadn't he said who the woman had been?

And then a different sort of worry began as she contemplated the incredible change in her life during the past few weeks. Now it was she, Laura, who was having the full-blown affair. Laura, who had always been silently disapproving of her friends' hectic love-lives. And was Laura really, *truly*, so very different now? If Karl hadn't proposed marriage she would still be going over to cook his supper, wouldn't she? But if Laura had been expecting to have Karl to herself the following Tuesday evening, events proved otherwise.

He phoned her from the airport to tell her he was back in Paris, and that a car would pick her up some time after seven. He had sounded rushed, remote, his voice belonging to the stranger in him that she had yet to meet. Was she being over-sensitivie, or was he beginning to change his mind?

But Laura told herself not to imagine things, and she was smiling brightly when the lift doors opened and she stepped out into his apartment.

He wasn't there to meet her, but there was someone else in the hall—a man about her own age. He was wearing a beige suit and his shirt collar was undone and the knot of his tie had been dragged halfway down his chest. He was on the phone, speaking rapid French. He turned round as Laura stepped into the hall and briefly smiled at her. But he was really listening to the person on the other end of the phone. He nodded, said yes, yes, and then rattled off again. And he was cross, insistent— and there was more than a touch of authority in his voice. Then he started talking about Stockholm and some shares ... And Laura blinked and followed the sound of more voices that were coming from the living room.

Karl was there. He was on the other phone, collar undone, tie pulled down like the other fellow out in the hall. And he was rubbing the back of his neck, nodding—he hadn't seen her. And there were dozens of

other people in the room! Well, four or five. All men.
All in various states of crumpled smartness. There were
documents on the table, a tape recorder, drinks. The air
was heavy with cigarette smoke. For a moment Laura
didn't know what to do, until Karl suddenly looked up
and saw her.

He smiled and her heart flipped over. Then he began
speaking in German, his voice crisp, cool—lethal, but
he was crooking a finger, making her cross the room,
and the men crouched over the papers on the coffee
table were suddenly standing up, running fingers
through their hair.

'I didn't know,' Laura whispered, coming up to him.

He put his arm round her, still speaking into the
telephone, then he broke off, kissed her, and mimed for
her to go and sit down.

Someone found her a drink, and she sat in one of the
enormous white leather chairs, trying to keep out of the
way, wishing that he had warned her. Now that his
colleagues had formally introduced themselves and
shaken her hand, they were back in conference again,
and it all sounded very high-powered.

The man from the hall appeared in the doorway and
called across to Karl, who interrupted his own
conversation and went outside to the other connection,
and she heard the strong authoritative tone of his voice
bring the conversation to an abrupt conclusion.

It went on like that for half an hour. There were
more phone calls, the whizz-kid out in the hall kept
coming backwards and forwards. One of the men on
the settee seemed to be a lawyer and was arguing about
the wording of a document, yet he seemed to be on
Karl's side. In fact, everyone seemed to be attached to
Rievenbeck's, yet they were fighting some long-distance
crises.

'Tell them we refuse to go beyond twenty million,'
Karl grated out at yet another request for assistance,
and Laura blinked and kept very quiet, because twenty
million in *any* currency sounded an awful lot of money!

It was an experience. As she sat there, East, West, North and Southern Europe seemed to parade before her eyes. And this was Karl's world, the world he moved and shaped in his particular way. How exciting! But she looked down at her simple Laura Ashley print skirt, her little camisole top and chunky cotton-knit short-sleeved cardigan, and thought for the hundredth time—but why me?

Eventually everyone left, then Karl came back into the living room, holding out a hand for Laura and leading her over to his desk where he sat down, pulled a document in front of him and picked up a pen. But he was still holding her hand.

'I didn't want you to find out this way,' he said. 'There were unexpected problems . . .'

'So I gather. But it doesn't matter,' she said. 'I already knew.'

'You did?' He looked—what?—suspicious?

'From Anthea,' she said.

'Oh.' But the tone of his voice hadn't changed.

'I wish you'd told me,' she added, and he let go of her hand and rubbed the back of his neck.

'I wanted us to talk—before. I intended taking my time with you, Laura,' and she felt irritated at being treated like a child. 'But the other evening things got out of hand,' he went on, trying to smile, but not quite succeeding.

Her face tightened. 'I told you then,' she snapped, 'this is the twentieth century—you didn't *have* to propose to me.'

Karl looked suddenly tired. 'Are you trying to tell me something?' he asked, and she turned away and wandered over to the sliding doors, pulling them open? All this cigarette smoke was making her feel sick.

'I don't know what I'm saying,' she said, feeling all the doubts and hurt of the day piling up on her.

'Why don't you go and get us some supper? Wasn't that what you came for?' And there was a little smile in his eyes that made Laura relent. 'I'll clear up in here,' he called, as she went through to the kitchen, 'and then I think I need a shower . . .'

Laura stood in the middle of the spotless, bare kitchen. What was the matter with her? Was it because she had expected so much of meeting him again? And even now that the others had gone, he still hadn't really kissed her. Was he that sure of her? Would all his other, more sophisticated women have been treated in this way? What about that woman in Rome? . . .

She sighed, cross with herself as well as with him, then opened the fridge—and stared! Then she checked the cupboards which were full of dinner services, coffee pots, tea cups—a regiment of glasses . . . But no food, unless you counted one egg, half a pound of butter and some coffee beans! So much for the international millionaire—he couldn't even organise supper!

Cross, hungry now, she marched through to the living room, and he wasn't clearing up, he was writing, obviously still deeply entrenched in the financial crisis of half an hour ago. What on earth would a few bits of food mean to him? Didn't he have enough to think of? Perhaps that was why he wanted to marry her—perhaps he was tired of always coming home to an empty larder.

He looked up, sensing her.

'There isn't any food,' she said, and he passed a hand slowly over his face.

'I'll phone for some Chinese—do you like Chinese?' then he laughed wearily and put the pen down and stared at her with those enigmatic blue eyes. His suntan had deepened; it suited him.

'Don't you want to carry on working——?' she began.

'Not now.' He pushed the paper away. 'It can wait.'

'How was London?' she asked, wanting to be interested, but not sure if he wanted to talk about his trip. 'I haven't been home since Easter.'

Karl looked curiously secretive; no, he didn't want to talk about it. 'Fine,' he muttered noncommittally. 'I was only there for one night.' Then he grinned, as if changing the subject. 'It rained.'

She pulled a face at him. 'It rained here, too.'

'And so in Brussels,' he admitted.

'So where did the suntan come from?' she asked.

'You noticed?' He was warming to her—coming back again.

'You bet I noticed,' she grinned.

He looked pleased. 'The suntan comes from Roma.' The Italian pronunciation gave his accent a sensual roundness, and Laura felt a moment's unease, as she remembered that woman again.

Karl stood up, caressing her arm lightly, stretching, saying he needed that shower, and she went out on to the terrace, not sure if she was wanted—feeling a little confused. Then she remembered that other visit to the flat, and it occurred to her that this time she had been sitting with a Mondrian hanging on the wall *without even noticing it*! Was that how it happened? Did you become familiar with the trappings of wealth so that they were—nice, but not important? And would she get used to Karl's international reputation, and all that implied, in the same way? She glanced around the roof garden, with its grass and fountain and tubs of coloured flowers, the table and chairs, the swinging seat ... familiar now ... and suddenly all her doubts fell away. Karl was what mattered. She and Karl and their love together. All—*this*—was part of him, and she would be a fool to think it didn't matter—but it was love, trust, understanding, and that indefinable something, that counted in a relationship. For richer or poorer ... wherever it was found. Love had to be given its chance.

It was as easy as that. She went back inside, slipping off her cardigan and walking through to the kitchen where she could hear him stacking glasses in the dishwasher. She stood in the doorway, looking at him— smiling at him—and he *knew*. He knew all about her fears, her secret dreads—he knew her as well as if he could look deep into her soul. It was exhilarating— frightening, and she swallowed as he dried his hands and threw the towel on the draining board.

'I'm not very hungry yet, are you?' he said, coming over and taking both her hands and lightly brushing his lips into her hair. 'Do you want me to phone for a meal yet?'

'Not really,' she whispered, closing her eyes and feeling her body awakening to the dangerous excitement of his latent strength.

'It's been a long time,' he murmured, nibbling her ear and easing one hand over her breast.

She leant into him, drowning in the soft darkness of her arousal, sliding her hands up and around his neck. The hair at his nape felt thick and soft between her searing fingers.

The top two buttons of her camisole top came undone. Then Karl unbuttoned her button-through skirt and it fell around their feet, revealing a full, voile petticoat trimmed with broderie anglaise. He liked it. He smoothed her thigh through the gossamer-soft material, while his lips plundered the yielding sweetness of her mouth.

'Let's go to bed—I have thought of nothing else,' and he was so convincing that she could almost believe him. Then he dragged his lips slowly down her neck while a few more little pearly buttons came undone. She could tell he was pleased she wasn't wearing a bra. 'Come,' he coaxed, knowing she didn't really need to be coaxed, and he was about to swing her into his arms when she suddenly remembered!

'I—can't,' she whispered, and he raised a quizzical eyebrow.

'But we both know you can,' he countered, 'beautifully.' Then he saw her embarrassment and the taunting light left his eyes, and his fingers gentled against her cheek. 'Ah—so this means you are not pregnant?' and she peeped up at him and nodded, her eyes full of shyness and regret for his spoiled homecoming. 'Never mind,' he said, 'there will be plenty of other times,' and for a moment she actually thought he was talking with disappointment that she wasn't already carrying his child.

He began kissing her again, and the last of the little buttons came undone. 'Karl—no, we can't,' she tried to remind him, watching the strain of passion on his face as he eased the fronts of her camisole open with one gentle finger. She looked soft, delicate, feminine in the lacy, Victorian-looking underwear—but beneath he saw the promise of a deeply satisfying fulfilment.

'There are many ways for a man and woman to please each other,' he said softly, his hands intimate, gentle, caressing, his sensual lips softening at her charming blush. He brushed against her and smiled at her intake of breath as those narrow, virile thighs demonstrated his need and attraction ... 'Come,' he coaxed again, 'let me begin to teach you ...'

Karl and Laura were married in Paris at the end of July, two weeks after Laura's twentieth birthday. The delay, if it could be called a delay, was because Karl wanted to take a week off for a honeymoon. 'We'll take a longer one later,' he had said.

It had been a crazy month when she had hardly seen him, except for his few flying visits to Paris, sometimes for only a night—and sometimes she could only meet him at the airport when he was passing through.

Laura had moved into the Rievenbeck apartment for the month before the wedding, and it was a good adjustment period. She needed time to get used to the idea of joining a family whose reputation and power spread beyond Europe and into America. She even became used to the Mondrian hanging above the fireplace; that was the best test of all!

Karl came and went, and she had to admit there were days of loneliness in the large apartment, punctuated by wild nights whenever he was in town. He had seemed disappointed again when she still wasn't pregnant, and Laura had suggested that they ought to be relieved and shouldn't she start taking the pill.

'You will do no such thing!' he had almost snarled, seizing her neck with a hand that was gentle, yet somehow menacing. 'If I had wanted only an affair I would have chosen an experienced woman.' And before she could even *think* what that meant, he added, 'I want you for my wife—for the mother of my children. Never forget it ...' and he had tipped her back into the pillows and made passionate, almost ruthless love to her. Which could have been because he hadn't seen her for nearly a week ... Yet, afterwards, lying in the warm darkness of near exhaustion, Laura decided that his reasons went deeper than that; reasons that were tangled up with the mystery of the man. The man she still didn't really know.

It was a simple civil ceremony. Karl had asked her if she had wanted a big church wedding, but that would have meant more guests, his family would have descended, and Laura wasn't sure if she was ready yet to meet them *en masse*.

He had told her about his family now. His widowed mother was Austrian and had moved back to Vienna where the Bank had its head office. In fact, most of the family seemed to be Austrian, until a shift in the border had slid them into Italy. Karl's home was in the Dolomites, and the image of him coming home to an empty town flat faded as he spoke. She would love it there—there was a lake. But he wouldn't say more. How typical of a man! From there he ran the offices in Milan and Rome, with near weekly visits to Vienna where a couple of uncles kept things ticking over. He had made it sound almost cosy and quite the most natural thing for a man to do. But Laura had discovered that he was the President of the company, and you didn't get that far advanced, even in a family business, unless you were brilliant, resourceful—and extremely tough.

Anthea flew in for the wedding from Nice, bringing the latest man in tow. 'We'll practically be neighbours,' she drawled delightedly, and Laura had the impression that her stepmother intended staying in Nice for quite a while! The girls from the flat came as well, of course, and a few people from Karl's bank. It was another hot day and Laura wore a simple silk dress in tiny blue and green sprigged flowers. It had a straight skirt and soft blouson top. She had bought it in Galeries Lafayette— very impressive, very expensive—made possible by the vast amount Karl was putting into her bank account on a regular basis.

'It is no more than convenient that you should have access to *our* money,' he had said, as soon as she had moved into the Rievenbeck flat. She had tried to protest; it still seemed strange taking money from him, and her feelings must have shown on her face, because he looked almost bored with the subject, and added, 'When we are married I shall be away a lot, Laura. Surely you see that it is sensible if you settle urgent bills when I am not there. It will take some of the pressure off me when I get back.' And although she felt pretty sure he was only using that as an excuse, she realised it would be rather insulting to refuse further. After all, it didn't mean she had to spend a fortune on herself. Or was that exactly what would be expected of Karl Rievenbeck's wife? What sort of an appearance would she have to keep up?

So she had bought the dress and accessories with only the tiniest twinge of conscience, and the look in his eyes when he had first seen it this morning had been worth all her doubts put together.

'You look beautiful,' he whispered, when the car came to collect them for the wedding, and Laura wished the golden day would go on for ever.

But it didn't. The ceremony was over all too quickly and they were outside again where the sun was shining through trees laden with heavy summer foliage. Colette was taking photographs; Anthea actually threw confetti and acted as if she was *pleased* at Laura's good fortune. Or did she see it as her own good fortune? ... And then Laura realised that someone else was taking photographs with a big, professional-looking camera, and there were two reporters with notepads. *Reporters!* One of them asked her in English if she had made the dress herself, and Karl had to scoop his new wife into the car before she had time to retort.

'Did you hear what she said?' Disbelieving green eyes widened angrily as she twisted round and stared as the little crowd on the pavement gradually receded. 'Does it *look* as if I made this dress? If she knew how much it cost . . .'

Karl was laughing gently, putting his arm around her. 'Don't forget they know you were an art student— perhaps they think you were studying fashion design.'

'But how did they *know* I was an art student? Why would they *care*?' and his expression had been half quizzical, half serious, and he had kissed her hand . . . but remained silent.

Laura gave a long, steadying sigh as they smoothly glided towards the hotel and wedding reception. Was her life always going to be filled with such surprises now that she was Karl Rievenbeck's wife? *Karl Rievenbeck's wife!* She sat silently staring past the driver's head. Everything was different now. The frivolity—the honeymoon, if you like—was over. Only now, in the next few weeks and months, would she discover exactly what manner of man she had really married.

CHAPTER FIVE

THE snow on the mountain peaks was painted a deep sunset red as the little private jet flew low through the narrow pass, giving its very special passenger her first, breathtaking view of Lake Ferno. Laura gazed incredulously over the pilot's shoulder; the plane had banked slightly to negotiate their twisting course, and then there ahead, as the pass opened up and they were finally through the mountain, lay the sapphire jewel of the bluest lake she had ever seen. The plane continued its descent, and the view was even better now; all around mountains rose steeply from the water's edge, where villas clung precariously to the thickly wooded slopes. There was a little town, a patchwork of warm orange roofs—a church spire—an island . . .

'It's beautiful!' she breathed, still in a dream; so much had happened since their wedding that morning. She wouldn't have believed it was possible to cram so much into one day.

They had flown by scheduled flight to Innsbruck, first-class, of course, and Karl had laughed at her enthusiastic excitement at the prospect. She supposed he had never travelled tourist in his life! And if that hadn't been adventure enough, a small lethal-looking private jet had been waiting at Innsbruck to take them south over the Brenner Pass and into Italy . . . Mountains, snow, hidden secret little lakes, steep valleys, mediaeval castles . . . Now they were in the Dolomites and Lake Ferno was coming up to meet them as the plane continued its circling descent.

For a moment Laura wondered where it was going to land, and then over the pilot's shoulder she saw a patch of level ground next to the town . . . there was a river— a golf course . . . They were skimming in low over the rooftops now, Karl checked her seat-belt, the airstrip was dead ahead and before it, on either side, were the banks of lights that controlled their glide path. Down and down—closer and closer. She held her breath, then there were the two gentle nudges. Safe. Laura sighed with relief, but made sure Karl wasn't aware of her slight apprehension. She was his wife now and would have to learn to be more sophisticated. He would expect that. In fact, somehow he seemed to be changing, now that he was almost home. He seemed to be resuming an identity that had never been a part of the Karl Rievenbeck she had met in Paris. She sensed his feeling of belonging, of responsibility—and it had more to do than with the running of his bank. Then Laura gave herself a mental shake. It had been a long day, she was tired and simply imagining things.

First class to Innsbruck, private jet to Lake Ferno . . . but the day wasn't over yet! A car was waiting for them, even Laura had expected that. But she wasn't prepared for it to take them down to the little harbour . . . and for a launch to be tied up alongside.

'I don't believe it,' she said, as their mountain of luggage was piled on board. 'You mean you live out there?' she queried, pointing across the lake where an island rose green and secluded amidst the still blue water and mirrored mountain peaks.

'It's a surprise,' Karl smiled.

'*Surprise!*' She wanted to hug him, but would Karl Rievenbeck expect such demonstrative behaviour from his wife in public? So she hung back, and when he helped her down into the launch she did nothing more than squeeze his fingers. It seemed to be enough; his blue eyes caught hers in a magic moment of their own.

'You look tired,' he said, brushing a finger across her cheek. 'It's been a long day—but I *had* to bring you straight here.' And along with the pride there mingled a touch of proprietorial right in the deep resonance of his accent.

The launch was cast off now, and they sat down as it

nosed its way between other boats and quietly thump, thumped towards clear, open water. Suddenly Laura had a strange sense of being snatched away from reality, away from the little town with its brightly coloured waterfront of cafés, hotels, full of colourful summer visitors—people—safety—All that was left behind as they headed out towards the cool green darkness of the island. For a moment she was caught between the old life and the new, and irrationally she had a desire to leap off the boat and swim for the shore. Only she couldn't really swim very well—and of course, she was being crazy.

Purposely she turned her back on the little town and her eyes rested on Karl, sitting comfortably in the bow of the launch, one foot resting up on the seat opposite, which accentuated the lethal, firm thighs. This is my husband, she whispered silently to herself. This tall, athletic man whose blue-eyed glance brought her alive, whose touch was reason enough for living, whose magnificent body drove her past the spiritual confines of this world and into a nameless timelessness where they would exist for ever . . .

A gentle breeze ruffled the smooth darkness of his hair, yet somehow he *was* different from all the times they had been together before. It wasn't her imagination. Now he was home, and she tried to remember what he had said about the Rievenbecks. The family, he had called them, with that special pride in his voice, and now she was part of that family, and it was obvious he wanted a child of their own pretty quickly. Why? Wasn't her love enough for a while? And why did he live high in the mountains in the middle of a lake, when surely it would have been more convenient to have lived in either Milan or Rome? *'But I had to bring you straight here,'* he had said. Why? She decided to ask him later, when they were finally alone.

'What do you mean, why have I brought you here? It is my home, Laura. *Our* home.' Karl was standing in the doorway of his dressing room, his jacket was off and he was in the process of removing his tie.

Laura was sorting through the drawers, trying to find where they had put her nightie; so strange having someone else unpack one's things. 'I—mean,' she shrugged, 'you made it sound important, that we *had* to come here tonight—our wedding night,' she added, 'instead of staying in Paris and coming on here tomorrow.'

'It's——' he searched for the right word, 'tradition.' His tie came off and he unfastened the top button of his shirt as he strolled into her room. *Her* room! That would take a bit of getting used to as well. 'The Rievenbeck brides always spend their wedding night in the castle.'

'*Castle?*' She stopped on her way to the dressing table, where *had* they put her nightie? 'What castle?'

He seemed surprised she should ask, as if *everyone* knew about the castle. 'You did not see the ruin—from the launch?'

Laura shook her head. But she had seen a notice nailed to a tree that had overhung the water. Two notices, in fact, both in German, Italian and English, and their message had been very clear. Private—keep off. Karl Rievenbeck was obviously possessive about his property.

'The castle was destroyed—it's a long story . . .' as he spoke his shirt came off and he strolled back into the dressing room. Laura was confused and tired; he hadn't told her about a castle . . . The Rievenbeck's castle! That meant they had to be an old-established, *aristocratic* family. She winced at the idea. Where *was* her nighdress?

'What's the matter, *liebling?*' he asked, coming in again, this time naked and in the process of shrugging himself into a towelling robe.

'I don't know what they've done with my nightie,' she said helplessly, and he simply padded over and pulled the bed quilt back—and there it was, a cloud of white, delicate lace. She sighed, cross with herself for not having thought of that, and awkward because he took

all this for granted. She went over and took the
nightdress.

He stopped her moving away, his hands gently
cupping her face. 'The strangeness will soon pass,' he
said seriously, and she remembered the Mondrian
hanging in the Paris flat, and tried to smile.

He went back through the dressing room to his own
bedroom and bathroom to take a shower, and Laura
undressed quickly and went into her own bathroom ...
but her little smile hadn't quite worked out, because she
guessed that Karl Rievenbeck, his family, and certainly
his villa, were going to take a bit more getting used to
than a painting.

She stood under the shower, cool and refreshing ...
the end of a magic day. Paris, the wedding, the first-
class flight, the private jet, the launch, the lake, the
villa ...

She had first glimpsed it through the island's dark
cypress trees. Karl had held her hand and they had
stood in the bows of the launch, holding on to a
guardrail. First she had seen a hotch-potch of red roofs,
all at different levels, the jagged outline etched against
the darkening evening sky. Then she saw the white
walls, shutters, balconies tumbling over with flowers.
Part of the house was a tower, another newer-looking
section overhung the lake, built on stilts planted in solid
rock. A terraced garden led up to the house, which
gradually became visible as the boat rounded a little
headland and came up to a jetty. There were lights in all
the windows, lights on the terrace, and someone was
hurrying along the jetty to welcome them.

People—there had been so many people, greeting her,
shaking her hand. A married couple looked after the
domestic running of the isolated estate, the husband,
Bruno, acting as a sort of butler-cum-valet, and the wife
as housekeeper. There were also a cook and a
kitchenmaid—and two housemaids, or whatever they
were called—two men to look after the gardens, a
carpenter and someone who looked after the boats.

Boats! And all of them smiling and welcoming her to
Monteferno. Until at last Karl had sympathised and
had led her into an elegant drawing room where behind,
out on the terrace, she could see their luggage being
carried indoors. Strange to think there was nothing
to do.

He had given her a whirlwind tour of the house, and
now all she could remember were the paintings and that
on all sides and from every window, she could see the
lake and mountains, the lights from the town, car lights
following the mountain roads ... Then he had brought
her up here and proudly opened the doors of her
bedroom. 'It has the finest view of the villa,' he had
said, and yes, the shuttered doors opened on to a
balcony which overhung the cool, peaceful waters ...
then he had shown her the dressing room, and beyond,
his bedroom. Her face had fallen and he had laughed.
'It is convenient—if I come home late, or if I work late.
But I do not intend spending much time there,' and he
had explained that hers should be the room they would
use.

They had dined by candlelight, after which the staff
had melted away, leaving them totally alone, absorbed
in the night and each other. After the simple lines of the
dress Laura had worn for their wedding, tonight she
had chosen a white, feminine, loose frothy blouse with a
tiered collar dipping low to reveal the swell of her
breasts. The skirt was of the same gossamer material,
the breeze flattening it against her legs, outlining the
contours of her body against the light from inside. Karl
had been pleased with her, as they had leant against the
parapet drinking their coffee and brandy, Karl smoking
his cigar. And when she thought there wouldn't have
been any more surprises left in the day, he brought out
a little box from his jacket pocket. It was a jeweller's
box, and inside was a pendant; a delicate twist of gold
surrounding a pearl, a warm, honey-coloured pearl the
colour of her hair. He put it round her neck and
fastened it, his fingers smooth and firm—reaching into

her hair. Then he kissed her as she fingered it; it was neat and simple—just right.

'Never wear diamonds,' he had whispered, 'you do not need them. I shall buy you pearls and gold, always . . .'

Now Laura stepped out of the shower, remembering, smiling, fingering the little pendant again, wrapping a thick white towel around herself. She probably would get used to people putting away her clothes and cooking her meals, and suddenly realised it would give her all the time in the world to paint.

A movement in the doorway made her turn round quickly. It was Karl—who else?—and his blue eyes were alive, bright, with little dancing devils. He was pleased at her absorption with the pendant, and she could tell he was pleased with the look of her, with her short, blonde, bubbling curls, the delicate arched brows, the big green eyes no longer shy, meeting his with sensual confidence that stirred the heat in him. She saw how pleased he was with her lightly tanned skin covering the feminine slope of her shoulders. The light shone on the little pearl between her breasts. He moved nearer, unwrapping the towel.

Laura reached up and kissed him, tugging gently at the belt of his robe, slipping her hands inside to smooth against the soft hardness of taut muscles, flat, iron-hard stomach . . . She eased the robe off his shoulders and both it and her towel slid to the floor, mingling in a crumpled heap, where they lay unwanted, forgotten, all night . . .

There was a phone ringing. Somewhere there was a phone ringing. Laura groaned; Colette would never hear it. And, eyes still closed, she rolled over, her feet groping for the floor. Then a strong, warm hand snaked around her bare midriff and a commanding voice murmured, 'Leave it.'

She fell back on the pillows, laughing at herself, snuggling against him, feeling him stir dangerously awake. 'But it's still ringing—it's in your room.'

'I said, leave it.' A leg snaked over her, trapping her, and his hand found a comfortable resting place on her breast. He drifted back towards sleep, enjoying the sensual drowsiness that followed a night of love. Laura smiled contentedly, knowing the day stretched before them without clocks or timetable. But the phone kept on ringing . . .

'Will someone answer it downstairs?' she whispered, sending a slow and caressing hand along his arm.

'No,' he murmured into her neck. 'It is a private line.'

'Then shouldn't you?' she insisted, because there was something urgent, important about an unanswered phone.

'I am not there.' He was properly awake now, raising up on his elbow, his knee smoothing the inside of her thigh. 'I like it here,' he smiled, pleased with himself as her eyes widened in delight. 'I have no wish to go in the other room when my wife is in this bed . . . I want you—now.'

'That's obvious, darling,' Laura whispered, her eyes shining as it all began again, this time slow and gentle, as he roused her with ease, yet she still shivered with delight at the fullness of his possession. There was no explosion this time—no passionate deliverance into another world. Instead there was an extra special sweetness as they lay side by side, relaxed, her leg flung over him, sharing a pillow, touching, kissing, together . . . The phone rang again half an hour later—but neither of them heard it this time.

The sun was shining full into the room when Laura woke up again. It was late, very late. Karl still lay in the deep drugged sleep of satisfaction. Over the bump of his shoulder and the dark, tousled outline of his head, she could glimpse a shimmering blue sun-sparkled lake. So, very carefully, she slid out of bed, slipping on the nightdress which had been so difficult to find, and which she hadn't worn in the end and slipped out on to the balcony, open-mouthed, stunned at the magical view waiting for her—bright sky, a blue lake, and a wide panorama of mountains folding one behind the other, all around. The sound of Sunday morning bells drifted enchantingly across the cool, blue stillness; faint, distant bells, tranquil—timeless. For a moment she stood and wondered how many Rievenbeck brides had heard the same haunting sound. How many Rievenbeck brides had stood on a balcony or a high castle keep, and seen every tree, every villa, every line of every mountain depicted with an overwhelming clarity?

A movement down on the terraces distracted her. Someone was setting breakfast for two, so she crept to the other end of the balcony, suddenly shy at being seen in her nightdress by a stranger. But they wouldn't be strangers for long. Soon they would have to get to know each other, and she would have to learn how to run Karl's home. She suddenly remembered the time when she had imagined his home was an empty apartment. What a long way she had come since then!

The phone began ringing and Laura realised she was outside the shuttered doors of Karl's room. If it kept ringing it would wake him. The doors opened easily, so she slipped into the cool, dark room, dark except for a ladder of sunlight streaking through the louvres and across the carpet to the large, immaculate, undisturbed bed. She took an impish pleasure in jumping right on to it, and stretching across for the phone, but before she could say a word, a woman's deep, sultry voice began, 'Carlo, *cara* . . .' and all the rest, in a long line of voluble, voluptuous Italian, was completely lost on Laura.

'*Un momento,*' she said, in a tight little voice, marvelling that probably the only two words she knew in Italian could actually be applicable. She put the phone down on the bedside table and padded through the dressing room to her own room. Karl was stirring in his sleep; she saw his hand go out and reach for her in the cool, empty space.

'There's a phone call for you in the other room,' and Laura tried to be nonchalant, but she had just remembered that she knew what *cara* meant. Dearest.

'Carlo', the woman had called him, Italianising and personalising his name to suit her own satisfaction. She wasn't a German-speaking local. Was she the woman from Rome?

She went through to her bathroom, closing the door, picking up the towel and his robe and turning on the shower. She didn't want to hear . . .

He was still talking when she went back to get dressed. Not really worrying what she wore, she picked out the green sundress that she had been wearing the first time they had met in the Louvre. It seemed a lifetime ago, but it was—what?—hardly two months. It would obviously take a little while for all the women in his life to discover he was no longer available.

When he came back into the room, she was sitting at the dressing table smoothing suntan cream along her shoulders. He stood in the doorway for a moment, tall, proud, naked. In the two months since she had known him his light summer tan had deepened to a golden bronze. *'The suntan comes from Roma,'* she remembered again, her stomach twisting with a new kind of pain. Yet, in the mirror, her eyes were full of the long, muscular length of him. He came across and stood behind her, taking the tube of cream and smoothing some across her back.

'It was a friend,' he began, and there was a stiffness in his voice, a stiffness in his hands. 'She said you should not have run away so soon, she speaks very good English.'

'I didn't know,' said Laura, looking at him in the mirror, but he kept his eyes down on her back.

'She has come up to the mountains for the summer. Rome is so hot.'

'Rome?' Her stomach flipped over.

'*Si* . . .' He was still wrapped up with the Italian language; still involved.

'Hasn't she left it a bit late?' Laura picked up a lipstick. Maybe she ought to put some cream on her face. 'It's the end of July.'

'Oh,' he shrugged, 'Eleanora travels everywhere—she is only now just back from Switzerland.' The flow of his English always disintegrated when he was tense.

'Eleanora's a beautiful name,' she managed to say, but he didn't comment.

'She has a villa up here near Morano—about half an hour's drive away.'

'So I expect we'll be seeing something of her,' said Laura brightly, as Karl screwed the top back on the tube and nodded, a tight, displeased sort of nod, before going to have a shower and getting dressed.

But the phone call and the elegant Eleanora—Laura just *knew* she would be elegant—faded from her mind during the next wonderful week; a week Karl had managed to keep free. They had moonlight trips in his big cruiser, out on the dark, star-studded lake. Or they relaxed on the smooth warm rocks around their pebbly beach. He had shown her the island; it had taken them all one afternoon to discover its cool green depths. There wasn't much left of the original castle. He didn't tell her what had happened, and Laura didn't like to ask. But it was old—mediaeval. Yes, the Rievenbecks went that far back!

They had swum naked in a hidden cove where the water was only a few feet deep. But he had warned her not to swim anywhere else because the water all around the island was very deep. Laura had shivered, some ancient, timeless, nameless fear chilling her bones. But only momentarily, for on other days he took her ashore and, like holidaymakers, they held hands and strolled the quaint narrow streets. There were flowers everywhere, on balconies, in tubs, tumbling out of the cracks in walls. There was a cable car, used by skiers in winter, but now the breathtaking, magically coloured rocks of the Dolomites rose in summer splendour all around her as they were carried higher ... and higher. There was still snow on the very top, but they couldn't go that far. Instead they walked through wooded paths, picnicked by waterfalls, watched the minute specks of hawks hovering above their heads in the deep, midsummer sky. It was a beautiful, memorable week, filled with new places, new experiences—and Karl. Nights of loving him, days of making love quickly, secretly, down on the warm rocks after their swim; on the soft turf in the castle ruins ... on a high, isolated corner of the mountain with the sun warm on his back ... But how quickly Sunday came round again—and then Monday morning.

Laura woke slowly, rolling over and reaching for him—but the rest of the bed was empty. Lord, look at the time—after nine! She was getting lazy. And then, struggling up, she saw the note propped against her bedside lamp. Karl had gone to Milan. He hadn't wanted to wake her. He wasn't sure when he would be back. Did that mean what time—or which day?

Missing him already, she was having a lonely breakfast on the terrace when Bruno brought out the telephone on a long extension lead. He found a space for it on the table, and ceremoniously lifted the receiver.

'The Contessa Eleanora Ferrara,' he announced with a little homely smile. It was a relief that one of the staff spoke some sort of English.

Laura thanked him, her heart suddenly down in her boots. The *Contessa*! Heavens, why hadn't Karl *said*? Why wasn't he here? She waited until Bruno had gone back indoors ... How did one address a contessa?

'This is Laura Rievenbeck,' she said instead, and her voice sounded calm and cool; how surprising!

'Eleanora Ferrara.' The voice was warm, voluptuous. 'It is so nice to speak to you at last, my dear Laura. I hope I did not get you out of bed this time.'

'Not at all,' said Laura, unsure what tone to adopt. 'It's nice of you to phone, Contessa.'

'Eleanora, please.'

'Eleanora,' Laura repeated. 'I'm afraid Karl is in Milan.'

'This is good. No? We do not always want the men around?' she prompted.

'I suppose not.' What a strange conversation! Laura transferred the receiver to her other ear. 'Is there anything I can do for you—Eleanora?'

'It is really I who is offering help,' the Contessa continued. 'Karl and I are such *good* friends,' a little laugh, 'and I know he would want us to be friends also. I know him—tell me, has he explained about the villa, about the staff? Do you speak German or Italian?'

'I'm afraid not,' Laura admitted. What should Karl have told her? What domestic arrangements did he imagine she would automatically make? Obviously all the women in his life had been able to control a place this size and a house full of servants—well, half a dozen or so, with complete ease.

The Contessa was making sympathetic noises at the other end of the line. 'We must talk—alone; men do not want to be bothered with such things. I shall come over. Today? Yes? For lunch, perhaps? We can have a *little* ...' she prounounced it slowly, conspiratorially, pausing a moment to think of the right phrase, 'we can have a little girl-to-girl talk. And I will help you with the party.'

'Party?' Laura's green eyes widened in dismay. 'What party?'

'Oh, it is too bad, men are so thoughtless! The party to welcome the new bride.'

'But there isn't any need,' Laura interrupted. 'I don't need a party—really.'

'But it is expected, my dear Laura.' A slight reproving chill mingled with the words, and then she brightened again. 'But you must not worry—I shall help you organise everything. I see you later, yes? About one o'clock.'

'Yes—fine,' Laura muttered, saying goodbye and slowly putting down the phone. Really, she ought to be grateful to have another woman to talk to; to explain things. And this was the Contessa the same person who had been entertaining Karl when he had phoned Laura in Paris? Surely Rome was filled with such women—

surely he had many women friends ... It didn't make
her feel any better, but common sense told her that she
couldn't go on avoiding them all for ever. Neither could
she go on avoiding her responsibilities. So instead of
ringing for Bruno, she went down to the kitchen to find
him.

There was a surprised silence when she eventually
found it and walked in. The cook was taking bread out
of the oven, one of the maids was over by the sink. It
was a lovely bright, half modern, half old-fashioned
room, but it was hot—there was no air-conditioning
down here. She would have to speak to Karl.

Laura smiled, and they smiled back. Silence. 'Ah, the
Contessa ...' Oh dear, what was the German for
'coming to lunch', but someone had the bright idea of
calling for Bruno, who interpreted, and the cook
nodded and smiled again, handing Laura a list of
menus which were in German, of course, and might just
as well have been double-dutch. Then Bruno's wife
arrived, the housekeeper, smiling and obviously talking
about today's lunch—nattering on and on, and it all
went over Laura's head.

'My wife says she knows what the Contessa likes and
she will—approve the meal for today, until you are
familiar ...'

Laura breathed more easily, but noted with a qualm
that the Contessa must be a pretty regular visitor.

'My wife also wishes to know when your maid will be
arriving,' Bruno continued, 'and if you wish her to have
the usual room on your floor.'

The whole room waited in silence for Laura's answer,
and she thought of the Contessa and all the worldly
things that were obviously expected of Karl's wife.
Should she have a maid? But what for? She took a deep
breath. This was her home, and her life, and they would
have to get used to running some things her way.

She smiled at Bruno. 'Will you please tell your wife
that I do *not* have a maid—neither do I require one.'
His face was deadpan as she added firmly, 'And if that

makes things difficult for the rest of the staff, then she must let me know. And will you thank her for coping with lunch? I'm sure whatever she chooses will be fine.'

Then she gave them all what she hoped was a 'I'm sure we'll get on well if we help each other' sort of smile, before leaving them to get on with their work.

Phew! What would they make of that? Laura hurried along the passageway so that she shouldn't hear the outburst or uproar, if there was going to be one. But she had been fair, hadn't she? Okay, so she wasn't used to this kind of life, but she was going to have to make the best of it. She ran up the stairs, suddenly giggling to herself. And they were going to have to make the best of her. She bet they had never envisaged the new Rievenbeck bride being a penniless English art student. The Contessa Eleanora Ferrara would be more in their line.

Laura spent the rest of the morning painting. In shorts and tee-shirt, and a floppy straw hat, she set up her easel and sat in the shade, beginning the outline of the mountains and the jagged edge of the lake. Blobs of colour made the little sailing boats; it was a new, fresh style for her. More blobs for the little town; it was more like a hasty sketch than a painting . . . she was totally absorbed for a good hour . . .

Bruno brought her a jug of her favourite ice-cold lemonade, so she guessed they were all still speaking to her in the kitchen. She sipped the drink that he had placed on a little folding table that he had brought with him. And now he stood behind her, arms folded over the suggestion of a middle-aged spread, staring critically at the painting, as she was herself.

'You take the gift from your mother?' he suggested, and Laura was so surprised, she swung round and stared up at him, having to hang on to her hat.

'How did you know? Did Karl tell you?'

He shrugged, busying himself with an imaginary speck of dust on the sleeve of the white jacket he wore in the mornings. 'The gift must come from somewhere,' he said vaguely, and then assuring himself that she didn't require anything else, he strode briskly back up to the terrace. But Laura stared after him, puzzled, certain that Karl must have mentioned something to him. But what was wrong with that? Why keep it a secret?

But there was no answer, so she returned to her painting, having promised herself to go back indoors and change soon after twelve. But it wouldn't take a minute just to finish this sky ... and that reflection was perfect—if she added a bit more white ... Time vanished until, at last, she heard the clip-clop of high heels coming down the steps.

She jumped up, eyes widening at the incredible vision coming towards her. Italian women were renowned for their elegance, and Eleanora Ferrara was no exception. Her shirt-style dress was red silk, superbly yet simply cut—spelling quality. As a condescension to the trip across in the launch, a matching scarf was tying back a heavy coil of thick, dark, Latin hair. She had dark brows, magnificently arched, good bones, a generous mouth. And a figure that made Laura feel like a scrappy schoolgirl.

'Good heavens, Contessa, I had no idea of the time!' Flushed, and hating herself for it, Laura made a supreme effort of meeting Eleanora Ferrara with a composed smile. 'I'm dreadfully sorry I wasn't at the jetty to meet you,' and she held out her hand, aware, too late, that it was smudged with paint.

The Contessa missed nothing. Dark, luminous eyes took in the tall, slim, blonde-topped figure, the minuscule shorts and tee-shirt that had never seen the inside of a couturier's salon. She saw the cast aside floppy straw hat with motheaten paper flowers around the brim ... and slowly her lips parted in a satisfied smile. She pretended not to see the outstretched hand, swooping automatically to kiss Laura on both cheeks.

'Now you have answered all our questions,' she began, holding Laura at arm's length, the more easily to study her. 'We all wondered why darling Carlo had been in such a rush to get married, but you are charming—quite charming—and so *young*,' she added, with a touch of—what?—amusement or spite? 'It is so lovely to meet you at last. I'm sure we are going to be good friends.' Then those eyes flicked over Laura again and she purred. 'Darling Carlo is such a very fortunate man.'

Laura muttered something polite, picking up a turpsy rag to wipe off her fingers. 'Do let Bruno get you a drink while I change,' she said, leading the way up the terrace steps, and somehow saying what was necessary until he came. But all the while her heart was growing colder, because you didn't have to be a psycho-analyst to read between the lines, nor to understand that special look in Eleanora Ferrara's eyes when she spoke Karl's name.

As she ran to get changed the certainty of the new situation ran with her. The Contessa and Karl had been lovers. The Contessa and the woman from Rome were the same person. Which of them had ended the affair—and when?

CHAPTER SIX

THE Contessa had stayed all afternoon, her voluptuous beauty slightly out of place in the mountains and lakes of the Alto Adigo, rather like an exotic hothouse plant in a meadow of wild flowers, Laura thought.

'You must allow me to advise you about your clothes. I hope Carlo is giving you sufficient allowance,' Eleanora said, her dark, sweeping eyes obviously disapproving of Laura's simple clothes.

Most of the time after lunch had been spent discussing the party. 'I will write you out a guest list,' she had suggested. 'But, naturally, you shall decide if you want them all to come. I will explain who everyone is—the list will take me several days. I will come back again, yes?' And then she had talked about clothes, and of course, Laura must have something made for the party and she, Eleanora, would introduce her to a genius here in Milano . . . And all the while Laura had smiled, nodded and agreed with her elegant guest, because there was no denying she was being helpful. Karl would expect his wife to move in the right circles, go to the right dressmakers, invite the right people . . . And she really ought to be grateful. Yet all the while she couldn't rid herself of the feeling of distrust. Was it natural for the ex-mistress to chat so happily with the new wife? It either meant that Eleanora hadn't minded losing Karl—or—that, even now, she hadn't lost him!

That was nonsense. Of course she had lost him; lost him as a lover, at any rate. But that didn't make it much easier for Laura, who didn't like the idea of Karl making love to this woman, of sharing the agony of joy he had shared with herself. She was jealous. It was a new experience for her.

But as she had eventually waved the Contessa

goodbye from the little jetty, it occurred to her that any woman in her right mind would be jealous of the elegant Italian whose poise and confidence would attract any man.

Laura had wandered back up to the terrace and had poured herself another cup of tea. Only now had it occurred to her exactly how isolated she was out here on the island. No friends or family for hundreds, a thousand miles. And no husband either . . . A little later Karl had phoned to say he would have to stay in Milan overnight. He had wanted to know what Laura had been up to that day, and she had laughed a little too brightly and told him she had been entertaining.

'Who?' The single word crackled down the line, and when she had told him, he added, 'What did she want? Didn't you tell her I was away?'

Why was he so cross? Didn't he want her to see other people? Or didn't he want her to see this particular person? . . .

Now, in the exquisite clear light of the following morning, Laura remembered it all and told herself she had imagined Karl's annoyance. And perhaps a woman like the Contessa gave the appearance of being the mistress of any acceptable man. She had been wearing plenty of rings, and was obviously married with a Conte tucked away somewhere.

Laura was strolling along the little shingle beach, the clear outline of the surrounding mountains reflected in the bluest blue of the lake. Sailing boats were out again, a little cluster of colourful specks weaving together out beyond the headland. She sat down on a large rock and watched them, noticing a little yacht, with blue and white sails, had left the others and was heading this way. She watched as it tacked nearer. It was really only a dinghy, with one man on board. And before long it was clear that he intended to come ashore—hadn't he seen the Keep Off signs? He had chosen a good spot. In fact, this was the only shallow beach on the island, the one Karl had shown her. The rest of the island rose from the lake with steep, rocky cliffs; it was a veritable fortress.

The dinghy was heading straight inshore now, its owner obviously believing he had the place to himself. You couldn't see the villa from here, and Laura wondered if she ought to go and tell him this was private property. But what the hell, it was a big island, there was plenty of room for both of them. In fact, it would be rather nice to have someone to talk to.

The sail suddenly went slack and started flapping about. The man jumped over the side into the shallow water and pushed the little dinghy right on to the beach; it made a damp, scratchy noise over the shingle.

He looked nice—youngish, twenty-five or six, she guessed, about her own height, and he was very dark, an almost olive skin tanned even deeper, and a sleek cap of black hair. He was wearing white swimming trunks that set off the long-legged litheness of his figure. He was a sportsman, used to exercise, but he didn't have the breadth or power of Karl, and he must have been shorter than her husband by nearly six inches.

As she watched in the shadow of her overhanging rock, he stretched and flexed his arms, idly gazing round the cove and casting a quick glance in the direction of the villa. So did that mean he knew his way around here? Next he rummaged in the boat and brought out a towel and a picnic hamper . . . and with impish delight Laura waited for him to get everything unloaded, before sliding down from her hiding place and strolling over.

He spun round, surprise then unashamed delight on his face as he took in her slim, bikini-clad figure. He began a torrent of Italian—from his tone she guessed he was apologising for trespassing, flattering her—and asking for forgiveness.

'Do you speak English?' she began, looking into his dark, rather beautiful eyes, and getting the feeling she had met him before.

He threw up his hands in delight. '*Si*—yes, you will

not send me away?' he implored again. 'I want only to
lie in the sun, and later to have some lunch. Perhaps
you would join me?'

Laura shook her head, remembering she was Karl's
wife and shouldn't really be encouraging an intruder.
'You had better go as soon as you've finished—I'll
pretend I haven't seen you.'

He protested with sorrowful, misty eyes and the
promise of an excellent wine ... and although she
laughed at his assumed distress, she noted a hint of
wicked humour in his voice and decided he would
probably be good fun, good company. But after only a
slight hesitation, she left.

Laura didn't give the incident another thought, until
the following morning at breakfast on the terrace. Karl
had phoned again to say he would be away for several
more days. All hell had broken loose and he was having
to fly on to Vienna. The king-size bed had seemed
lonely without him, but now, as she sipped her orange
juice and decided to continue with her painting of the
lake, she saw the boats again, and then the blue and
white sails of the little dinghy.

Maybe she would have that swim after all. On
impulse, she raced back to her room, changed into a
bikini, and remembering to leave her rings safely on the
dressing table, she gathered up sun-hat, towel, sun-
cream and dark glasses. She shouldn't be doing this, of
course, Karl wouldn't approve. But it didn't mean
anything, and how many attractive women would he be
meeting in Milan and Vienna? She suddenly thought of
the Contessa and was pleased that she was here in the
mountains instead of somewhere loose with Karl.

The dinghy was already pulled up on the beach by
the time Laura arrived. At first she pretended to be
surprised and a bit cross that their private beach had
been invaded again, but he gave her a cheeky grin,
holding out his hand in introduction. His name was
Tonio de Vito.

'This is the only place on the island where I can

swim,' said Laura, without giving him her name. 'It's too deep everywhere else,' and he promised not to speak or come anywhere near her, and moved his towel and picnic basket to the far side of the little cove, which wasn't exactly what Laura had planned—but there wasn't much she could do about it.

Thirst got the better of them both. After a short swim and an hour or so of sunbathing, Tonio came over to offer her a long, cold drink, and she was very pleased to accept it. So they put their towels near each other in the shade, and sipped iced, minty tea which was quite delicious and refreshing.

Tonio told her about himself. He was on holiday, staying with a relative for a few weeks. Normally he was a racer of fast boats—powerboats—and fast women, Laura added silently to herself. Yes, there was conceit behind the charming smile, and he probably slayed girls at his feet. Yet she liked him. It was better to be here than wandering around the villa worrying about Karl.

'Why aren't you racing now?' she asked.

He stared out across the lake. 'I had an accident with my boat—I need a new one——' He smiled down at her curiously. 'And such things are expensive, *very* expensive.'

There was a strange little silence and Laura wasn't quite sure how to react. Then after a few minutes, he added, 'It is lonely for you—with your husband away?' and she felt guilty and said quickly that she didn't have time to be lonely because there was so much to learn and she had her painting.

Again he invited her to share his lunch, and she was almost tempted to agree, when she suddenly remembered that if she didn't turn up at the villa everyone would be worried. 'But if you're coming again tomorrow, I'd love to have a picnic then. I'll tell Cook to organise something, she's bound to pack far too much.' But he couldn't come next day, so they settled for Friday instead, always supposing Karl wasn't back.

'But of course,' he smiled, his dark-lashed eyes slowly

lingering over her scantily clad figure. 'If the husband is at home I keep well out of the way.'

Laura felt suddenly flustered. She hadn't meant it like that. 'I—may not be able to come, anyway,' she said, gathering up her towel and things. But he only smiled, a gleam of white teeth in his olive skin, and she had felt distinctly uneasy as she made her way back to the villa.

She had a shower before lunch, and afterwards, in a simple cotton sundress in a pretty flowery print, she sat at the dressing table and fingered her damp blonde curls into place. She was getting quite a tan now, a sort of golden cornflake colour. It suited her. She slipped on her rings, gave her curls another tussle—they would soon dry on the terrace—and she was halfway downstairs before it occurred to her that she hadn't been wearing her wedding ring on the beach that morning—and yet Tonio had known she was married!

It was really hot today, and Bruno had set her lunch in the dining room, which was in the newer part of the villa projecting out over the lake. Air-conditioning won a battle with the sun streaming through the picture window . . . Laura was pleased with his thoughtfulness, she really ought to ask Karl if they could get air-conditioning down in the kitchen.

But she ate her meal slowly and thoughtfully, thinking about her ring—and Tonio . . . But the whole town probably knew Karl Rievenbeck had married an English girl. Yet Tonio wasn't a local. Oh, what did it matter? . . .

It was a good thing that Laura hadn't arranged to meet her intrepid dinghy sailor the following day, because halfway through Thursday morning, when she was tackling her painting again, the Contessa telephoned to say she had the guest list ready and would Laura like to see it later that day?

'Are you sure it's not too much trouble?' asked Laura, from the extension out on the terrace. 'Would you like me to come over to you? Tomorrow morning, perhaps?' Which would give her a good excuse not to meet Tonio.

'No, no. Tomorrow I am—er—lunching with a friend,' Eleanora said a little too hastily. Which friend? Karl? Laura put the idea instantly out of her mind. 'I will come today, then we will have to decide on the menus. Naturally you will have to hire extra staff...'

So the Contessa came, and this time Laura was at the jetty waiting for the launch which had been sent over to meet her car. What an incredible way to travel! Laura still couldn't get used to it.

It was mid-afternoon, and they had tea on the terrace, Laura's favourite blend which Karl had ordered specially for her. Eleanora looked even more ravishing today in a bright blue, backless, practically frontless dress, with the designer's emblem exaggerated in candyfloss pink stripes around the hem. The bold design accentuated her rounded, voluptuous shape. Men might *look* at slim girls, but it was always the ample armful they preferred.

'I have the list—here,' she said, unfolding an enormous sheet of paper from the minute confines of her bag.

Laura tried not to look shocked. 'How many's there?' she muttered.

Eleanora shrugged. 'One hundred—one hundred and twenty. I forget exactly.'

'I'm amazed you know so many people,' Laura admitted, realising as she saw the older woman's little smile that such a remark sounded extremely naïve. Her eyes ran down the list until she eventually reached the *Contessa Eleanora Ferrara*. But there was no Conte. 'Isn't your husband coming?' Laura asked, assuring herself first that Eleanora was wearing a wedding ring.

'Benito died three months ago,' the other woman answered.

'Oh, I'm sorry.' Why the hell, thought Laura, can't I learn to keep my big mouth shut?

'It does not matter.' And seeing Laura's shock,

Eleanora added quickly, 'It was expected for some time. My husband was—much older than I. It was a marriage of—convenience, I believe you say.'

'Yes ... Do you have any children?' Laura asked, trying to make amends.

Eleanora laughed. 'Do I look like a mother?' and seeing the younger girl's discomfiture, she added, 'But there are compensations, believe me. As you will one day discover for yourself.'

'I'm not sure I understand,' said Laura in a frosty voice that surprised even herself.

The Contessa smiled rather nastily, and the dark eyes flashed with a touch of spite. 'Do you really believe all this will last?' she asked, gesticulating with long, expressive fingers. 'All this love—this honeymoon. Do you imagine it will always be so?'

'No—of course not,' Laura began, not really knowing what to say. 'I know things change . . .'

'Do not be hard on yourself,' Eleanora interrupted. 'You are young and healthy. It is natural, no? You enjoy having a man in your bed. And Carlo is good, yes, very good, very experienced, very—how do you say?—virile?'

'I really don't think . . .' Laura tried again, feeling the blush darken her cheeks . . . But the Contessa was all contrite.

'My dear Laura, forgive me, but I assumed you knew that Carlo and I . . .' The rest of the red-hot sentence was left to hang in the air.

Laura coughed, her throat suddenly dry. 'I—did get the impression that—you and my husband . . .'

'Ah, good—I thought so.' Eleanora sighed with relief. 'Naturally, you would not have expected a man like Carlo to have been . . .?'

'Celibate?' Laura offered.

'*Si*, celibate.' She laughed at the very idea. 'And as my own husband was not very, shall we say, *attentive*, then these little arrangements are made.'

Laura sipped her tea, her hands trembling. 'How long

have you known Karl?' she asked. What she really
wanted to say was, 'How long did the affair last?'

'We met when he lived in Roma, before his father
died,' Eleanora reminisced. 'I was a young bride, about
your own age, already disillusioned. I had married to
please my family, you understand,' she explained
crisply, 'and to please myself in some respects. But I
soon learnt that a woman needs more than wealth and
a title. Carlo was . . .' she gave the superb Italian shrug,
'he was so—*simpatico*. But he has changed a great deal
in ten years. We both have.'

'Are you saying that—that you've been Karl's
mistress all this time?' Laura's green eyes were wide
with astonishment and dread.

'What else did you expect?' Dark, eloquent,
groomed eyebrows were instantly raised.

'I mean, right up to this summer—after your
husband's death?'

'Why should we stop seeing each other when Benito
died?'

'And when Karl came to Paris?' Laura almost
squeaked, and the Contessa's eyes hid a secret smile.

'In Paris he met you, and he was quite right—you will
make the perfect mother for his children, for the proud
Rievenbeck heirs,' she added with almost a shiver, and
Laura felt her heart grow cold. The mother of his
children. It was the same expression Karl had used; it
almost sounded as if they had planned it together. 'And
that is why I do not want you to get hurt,' Eleanora
continued, her sudden displeasure passing. 'You are
young—inexperienced. I am certain you were a virgin
before you met Carlo . . .' Laura couldn't meet her eyes,
and it was the only answer she needed. 'Precisely. You
were perfect. And believe me, Carlo honours his
responsibilities. As his wife, as the mother of . . .' she
saw something in Laura's eyes and broke off. 'You will
be rewarded with all this, for the rest of your life,' she
continued, gesticulating towards the villa, then the
lake—the mountains. Then the sensuous mouth

thinned. 'But it would be a mistake to imagine you can keep Carlo satisfied for very long. When the novelty of your inexperience has passed, it will be only natural that he should look elsewhere; but discreetly, you understand. And then it will be time for you to arrange a little liaison of your own.' She stopped at last as Laura clattered down her cup and saucer on the table.

'And presumably you're happy to wait around until that day comes, so that you can resume your affair with my husband? I think you had better leave, Contessa.' Hot anger burned from Laura's eyes.

'My dear child, did I say such a thing? Calm yourself. Carlo may not stray for a year, maybe two. And I can assure you I am not prepared to wait that long. Come,' she said briskly, as if she had been spending the last half hour discussing their wardrobes, 'we have wasted enough time—where is that guest list? I will tell you who everyone is . . .'

Laura was so dumbfounded at the woman's icy calm that she meekly handed over the list and listened to what Eleanora had to say, not that she would remember a word of it. But eventually her rage calmed and her voice sounded more normal as she asked one or two questions. And at long, long last Bruno came to say that the launch was ready to take the Contessa ashore. She had ordered it for six o'clock and it was nearly that now.

'And we still haven't discussed the food—or your dress—but at least we have decided on a date.'

'If that's all right with Karl,' Laura reminded her.

Eleanora laughed. 'But of course, *everything* must be all right with Carlo,' and she hugged Laura goodbye and said she had had a lovely afternoon . . . which was a lot more than Laura could say.

It was almost dawn before she finally fell into a restless, uneasy sleep. A sleep dappled with visions of Karl and Eleanora . . .

'You are very silent.' Tonio poured himself more wine,

then glanced at Laura's firm profile as she gazed out across the lake. They had just finished a superb picnic lunch, sitting in the shade of a cypress tree. Yesterday she had almost decided not to keep their rendezvous on the beach. But the Contessa's revelations, and her own restless night, had produced a spirit of reckless anger. Wasn't this just the sort of relationship she would one day have to cultivate if Eleanora Ferrara had her way?

'I was just thinking, that's all,' she shrugged, reaching into the picnic basket for a peach.

He passed her a fruit knife. 'Someone has upset you?' His smile was friendly, sympathetic—cagey?

'No.' Laura began slicing her peach.

'You are wondering what your husband is doing in Vienna?'

'How do you know he's there?' she asked in surprise.

He shrugged, stretched out on his towel and studied his big toe. 'You told me—the other day.' Had she? Then he rolled on to his stomach and propped himself up on both elbows. He smiled up at her, his beautiful Latin eyes reminiscent of long, hot summer nights . . . 'If you are missing him, I would willingly . . .' and he stretched out and gently smoothed the bare skin above her elbow.

'*Tonio de Vito!*' She slapped his fingers with the flat of the little knife and he screamed as if in agony, rolling over, legs in the air, making a dreadful fuss . . . Then he began laughing and Laura began laughing, and in the end he caught her hand and said how about a trip out in his boat? 'I'm not a very good swimmer,' she confessed, and he laughed at her lack of confidence in him, but added quite seriously that it would only be a gentle sail. But if they *did* capsize, he, Antonio, would rescue her and carry her away to his secret cavern where they would live blissfully for ever . . . and she laughed at his romantic flamboyance, and wondered what on earth he was doing wasting his time with her.

But she agreed to go—and it was gorgeous. At first the boat seemed to heel at a dreadful angle, until Tonio saw her nervousness and slackened the sail until they were more or less level on the water. He didn't take her far—hardly beyond the headland of their little cove, but it was enough to get the breeze through her hair and to feel released—free. He let her take the tiller, sitting close beside her, his leg brushing her own, his face turned up in concentration on the set of the sail. It was strange how his physical contact meant nothing to her, and she began to wonder again why a man like Tonio was wasting his summer up here on the lake; shouldn't he be trying to get himself another boat?

She asked him about it, if there was a chance of his racing again this season, but he seemed hesitant to talk about it, muttering only that he hoped to get a new boat shortly, but that nothing was definitely arranged.

Then their conversation had to stop as a little gust of wind hit the sail, and this time when they heeled over, Laura didn't mind so much. In fact, as the little dinghy picked up speed she found it quite exhilarating. Little waves splashed over the bow, and a light spray dampened her face. Then the gust slackened, their speed dropped and they were horizontal again.

To get back to the beach they had to tack in a dog-leg, ducking under the boom as it swung across. But all too soon Laura noticed they were almost back to the beach. It had been lovely, a real treat. And she jumped into the shallow water with Toni and helped him pull the dinghy ashore.

'That was super—really,' she began, and he was pleased, but—what?—uncertain about something. One moment he seemed attracted—too attracted—and the next moment it was as if he felt guilty about being here.

'I have to go now,' he said, pushing the boat out again almost immediately, while Laura stood and watched him sail away, frowning at his behaviour, and feeling a little lost, as if her only contact with the outside world was slipping away. Then she gathered up the picnic basket and her own swimming things, but somehow didn't feel like going back to the villa for a while.

So instead she wandered near the water's edge, scrambling between trees and over rocks . . . making her way back to the house the hard way. Eventually she came to the boathouse near the jetty, and she wondered if there was a little boat she could take out herself, maybe something with a little outboard engine. But everything was locked up, and there was no sign of the boatman. He was probably sleeping off a hot August siesta. Pity—it would have been nice to go out on the lake again. Maybe even over to the little town she had visited only briefly with Karl. She had a sudden urge to wander through streets and see shops and people. She walked along the slatted boards of the jetty and stared out across the lake to the clear, pin-sharp outlines of hotels and a church steeple. And despite the heat, she shivered. So silly to feel suddenly trapped.

She wandered up the terrace steps, having planned to spend the rest of the afternoon with her teach-yourself-German book. Perhaps she ought to find a private tutor, someone in the town; some reason for her to go across regularly.

Bruno met her at the top of the steps and took the empty picnic basket. Karl had phoned at lunchtime to say he would be home again that night.

'He regretted you were not here to speak to him,' Bruno added. Laura's eyes slid away from his face. 'And he says he may be very late—so do not wait up for him.'

But she stayed up until gone midnight, feeling somehow restless, uncertain. Looking forward to seeing him again—but . . . Oh, it was all Eleanora Ferrara's fault. She had planted doubts, grave doubts. Now Laura needed Karl to be here, in her arms, telling her everything was all right, assuring her of his love . . . But he wasn't here, and it was half past twelve, and Bruno was still wandering about.

'Do you normally wait up this late?' Laura asked, as Bruno came through the drawing room to check that the sliding glass doors were locked, and he told her there was no need for either of them to wait up any longer, because sometimes Karl did not get back until four or five in the morning.

So Laura went reluctantly to bed, reading until nearly two, but then Karl still hadn't come, so she switched off the light and was soon asleep.

It was full light when she awakened and automatically stretched out her hand across the large bed. But the sheet was smooth—empty. He wasn't there!

There had been an accident. Laura sat bolt upright in sudden panic. The little jet had crashed in the mountains. Why hadn't anyone woken her?

She was halfway to the door, grabbing a robe to cover her nakedness . . . when she suddenly remembered that Karl had his own bedroom and there was just a very slight chance . . .

Holding her breath, almost too scared to go and look, Laura tiptoed through the adjoining dressing room and quietly opened his door. She peered round— and the relief was so great that she felt sick. Karl was there, lying on his stomach, arms flayed out in exhaustion, the duvet covering only up to his waist. The strong shape of his bare shoulders and back brought their own response deep inside her, even now.

She sighed softly, the sickness passing. Why had he come in here? She wouldn't have minded being disturbed. Minded! Heavens, she would have welcomed it. She had an overpowering urge to go across and kiss him—but no, he must be exhausted; she shouldn't wake him. But it didn't seem right, however tired he was, for him to spend the night in here, under the same roof but in separate beds . . . then like a devil, Eleanora's words returned to torment her. *'It would be a mistake to imagine you can keep Carlo satisfied for very long.'*

She stood in the doorway for ages, staring at him, her mind in a turmoil, remembering all her early doubts about why a man like Karl should want to marry a little nobody like herself. She remembered Anthea's disbelief—incredulity. Everything had happened so quickly . . .

There was a movement in the bed, as if he was suddenly aware of somebody's presence. Laura backed out hurriedly, knowing she had to get away and think . . . But the door wasn't quite closed when she heard him roll over and mutter sleepily, 'Eleanora? El-ean-ora . . .?'

CHAPTER SEVEN

'No, it isn't Eleanora—it's me,' said Laura, bursting
into the room and sending the door crashing back
against its stop. 'Remember? You married me in a weak
moment a fortnight ago. But don't worry about the
Contessa, she practically *lives* over here these days. I'm
sure you'll get together again before very long.'

'Laura . . .'

But she didn't wait, flouncing out of the room just
as the duvet was thrown back and Karl sprang out of
bed. She ran through the dressing room and into her
own room, but he was right behind her, tall and
naked, catching her arm—but she twisted out of his
grasp.

'Laura, *liebling*,' he tried again, and he was angry,
but an anger touched with amusement, if such a thing
were possible. 'I did not mean . . .'

'Of course you didn't,' she rounded on him, clutching
the fronts of her robe together. 'Very silly mistake—but
don't worry, I know all about it.'

'All about what?' The blue eyes were cool now, the
strong lines of his face etched in firm disapproval. No,
this wasn't how he expected his wife to behave. He had
chosen a young, inexperienced, *doting* wife and had
expected her to be quietly submissive while he carried
on his wild affairs. Was Eleanora the only one? How
many others did he have in Milan and Vienna?

'I know all about your affair with Eleanora Ferrara,'
she said stiffly, raising her head to glare him right in the
eye. 'And you've been gone five days—aren't you going
to ask me if I'm pregnant, then as soon as I am you
won't have to bother with me again!'

The sensual curve of his mouth had thinned with
distaste. 'It is not yet time for you to know,' he said,

and his perfect knowledge of her body made her even more annoyed.

'But you aren't denying that's why you married me, are you?' she taunted. 'Right from the beginning, in Paris, when you came back from that first trip—even then you *hoped* I was pregnant. Answer me!' she demanded recklessly, amazed that she was speaking to him in this way. 'Answer me—that's why you married me, isn't it?'

He turned away from her and she stared at the long line of his naked back, tanned a deep bronze now, except for a tantalising white strip. He ran long, expressive fingers through his dark ruffled hair; he didn't look sleepy and vulnerable, having just woken up; he looked strong, powerful, aggressive.

'If I had not wanted you to be the mother of my children ...' There was that expression again, she thought wildly, 'then I would not have married you,' he said, turning round and facing her again, and now the blue eyes were icy cold, cold as a frozen lake. 'And I believe I told you that in Paris, as well.'

Laura tossed her head. 'You—seriously thought you could bring me here as some reproductive machine, while your mistress is installed not half an hour away!'

'Stop it, Laura. I do not wish to hear you speak that way.'

'I bet you don't! Thought I'd sit at home and keep quiet. Well, you've got another think coming! I'm not staying here to be the laughing stock of the whole town. I'll leave right away.'

'You will not.' He moved swiftly across the thick pile carpet, grabbing her arm and practically sweeping her off her feet. 'You will never leave me,' and there was something frightening in his eyes, something more than the ancient Rievenbeck family pride. It was more like some special private anger that his chosen wife should dare to be dissatisfied.

'I'm not your prisoner,' she grated, trying to struggle

free, but it was useless. The fronts of her robe fell apart as she tried to twist away, and their bare legs tangled together. Desire licked across Karl's face as his eyes devoured her. Lord, she mustn't let it happen, not like this. But her body was responding to the hard, lethal shape of him . . .

'I didn't say you were my prisoner.' His voice shook. 'But you are my *wife*.'

'That doesn't give you the right . . .'

'It gives me *every* right. Laura . . .' The feel of his hands changed subtly. 'It's been six days . . .'

'No!'

'Yes!'

'It's not me you want—it's *her* you think of when you wake up. Well, okay, go to her. Only don't expect to find me here when you get back.'

'You don't mean that.' He was pulling the robe off her shoulders, half pushing, half carrying her towards the bed.

'No, Karl. You can't win every argument like this.'

'I'm not winning any argument. I want you—I have been away all week.'

'Yes,' she retaliated, giving an almighty shove and finally breaking free. 'Long enough to forget all about me. Long enough to think I was your mistress!' She purposely hadn't said *ex*-mistress, to see if he would correct her. He didn't.

'I was half asleep. The mistake was regrettable,' he said, taking a steadying breath, forcing himself to acknowledge the justification of her anger. 'Eleanora and I were together a long time.'

'Yes,' she interrupted. 'Ten years, to be precise. Long enough for any self-respecting man to marry her once she became a widow. That's what she expected,' she added, instinct telling her how she would have felt in similar circumstances.

'We all expect many things that do not materialise,' said Karl coolly, and Laura was so annoyed at his

raging calmness that she picked up a pillow and hurled
it at him.

'Swine! I suppose you'll say next that she wasn't the
only one.'

He tossed the pillow to the floor, taking a step
nearer, his lips twisting menacingly as she backed off.
'Ten years is a long time, naturally there were other
occasions . . .'

'Oh, naturally. Well, it might be natural for you—but
didn't you ever *consider* marrying her?' In the back of
her mind she recognised something crazy in the wife
fighting for the rights of a mistress. But somehow she
had to get to the bottom of his association with
Eleanora. What was there about her that made her an
unsuitable mother for his children? And why did she get
the impression that they had discussed the need for his
marriage—had somehow planned it together? . . . Did
that explain why he had married a little nobody within
a few weeks of their meeting?

'Of course I considered marrying Eleanora, even
before she was free,' Karl was saying now, and Laura
discovered that that wasn't the answer she wanted to
hear, either.

'Then why didn't you? I'm sure she would have made
a more suitable wife than I would.'

He grabbed her. Savage lips descended on her own,
strong hands ripped the broderie anglaise negligée from
her body.

They fought, Laura kicking and shouting at him to
stop, but it was like beating against an armoured tank.
He was so big and strong, and her own body felt slim
and fragile beside him.

'I'll tell you why I married you,' he grated, and his
breath rasped in his throat as desire mingled with the
anger on his face. And now she was tumbled across the
bed and he was towering over her, his body blocking
out the sunlight, her mind and senses filled with the
virile aura of male aggression.

'Get off me! I don't want you, Karl.'

'Liar!' His eyes gleamed as he fended off another blow. 'You want me, Laura. Now and for always—do not pretend.' And although she twisted and squirmed it was useless to fight him. But she must never give up—never. And so they rolled and tumbled, twisting together, her blonde curls haywire, writhing in an agony of self-deception. Oh how she hated him!

He kissed her again, savage, ruthless lips descending without mercy.

In a rage she bit him, and he pulled back with an angry cry, dabbing his mouth with the back of his hand.

'You should not . . .' he began, in an angry, icy whisper, but she had taken advantage of his preoccupation and had wriggled over to the edge of the bed. His hand shot out and pulled her back, and she saw with sudden shock a nick of blood on his bottom lip. 'You will apologise,' he said, his face white and livid. 'Now—before you move from this bed.'

Mutiny pressed her lips together.

'Laura.' The command was repeated.

'No. It was your fault.' But she was shaking now, really frightened, because everything had suddenly gone too far, and she hadn't meant to hurt him. In fact, such a thing seemed an impossibility.

'Do not make me do anything I might afterwards regret.' He shook her, and through his fingers she could feel a rage and passion burning him up. No woman treated Karl Rievenbeck this way. And if they dared to do so his punishment would be—what? She swallowed and tried to struggle out of his grasp. 'Laura,' his voice shook, 'you will apologise . . .' He licked his lip, and suddenly her face crumpled.

'I'm sorry—I didn't mean . . .' she sobbed, touching his face, and suddenly they weren't fighting any more, but were clinging to each other, and Karl was murmuring her name.

'You should have come to my bed—you should have woken me up like this,' he said, and now he was pressing her back into the pillows again, but this time there was need and love mingled with the desire on his face.

'And you should have come to bed—*our* bed—as soon as you got home,' she said firmly, and oh, everything was going to be all right and his hands were bliss on her body; coaxing, taunting, arousing—oh, how she wanted him!

'So that's why you were cross,' he taunted.

'No, it wasn't,' she insisted, but he was silencing her with lips that had forgotten their pain, silencing her with the hard smoothness of his body that was still strung with tension, and she gasped as his searching, intimate caress proved she was ready for him.

'Do you still want to know why I married you?' he asked, as their bodies drew remorselessly nearer.

'Yes, tell me,' she breathed, closing her eyes and breathing deeply in anticipation.

His knee nudged the inside of her thigh. '*This*——' he grated, 'is why . . .' and then their world revolved in the long excitement of his lovemaking, where spirit matched spirit, fire matched fire, until tension and aggression burned themselves out in a white-hot passion of mutual fulfilment . . .

Afterwards, in a deep sleepy haze, with the weight of his body still upon her, Laura smoothed his hair with slow, heavy fingers.

'Does that answer your question?' he murmured into her neck.

'Yes,' she whispered, but mingled with the dark, glowing warmth there still lay the irritation of suspicion. Had he married her because they were special together—or had he married her to get her pregnant? She wriggled beneath him, uncertain, desperately wanting him to love her for herself . . . and then she groaned as his body began stirring . . . and everything started all over again.

Laura wore the memory of this lovemaking like a warm

protection against a chill wind blowing off the mountains. Not that there was a chilly wind in reality, in fact, August shimmered in continual heat; but she needed its comfort and protection in this strange time of adjustment, when she had to learn that Karl could be passionate and attentive one moment, then a cool, ruthless, business man the next.

The rest of August developed into a strange period of limbo. There was a letter from Anthea one morning, posted in Nice, but including a French newspaper cutting of the photograph of their wedding.

Karl gave it a cursory glance as she passed it across the breakfast table. 'Your stepmother is well?' he asked, his cool politeness strangely accentuating his disapproval. He never talked about Anthea, in fact, Laura couldn't remember him speaking badly about anyone; he registered disapproval by a strong, almost tangible silence.

'She doesn't seem to be enjoying Nice,' Laura said, quickly scanning the two pages of irate writing. 'She says she's getting bored—she's thinking of coming on to Venice.' That was rather close to home; she looked up at Karl to see what he would make of it.

'If you wish to invite her here, then you must do so, Laura. She is your family. I do not forget it.'

But they let the matter drop. Laura didn't really want Anthea at Montiferno, and the long strange days of limbo continued while Karl commuted back and forth to Milan, busy as ever, caught up in the whirl of the financial empire of his own making. They didn't say any more about Eleanora; Laura tried to take each day as it came—and there were many little golden moments in those last days of August. Moments when he would reach sleepily for her in the middle of the night. Moments during their occasional shared breakfasts on the terrace when she would glance up and find his eyes warm upon her. Moments, as when she had been absorbed in her painting and he had found her, and been content to stay quietly watching as she put the last finishing touches to the view she had begun on their honeymoon.

'Tell me more about your mother's painting,' he had said, and she had described those six pictures that she would never see again.

'Bruno was talking about my mother, a couple of weeks ago,' she said. 'Did you tell him that she painted?'

Karl looked away. 'I may have done. What did he say?'

'Nothing.'

He kissed the top of her head. 'You are a very talented young lady—I am proud of you,' and for a while they had been close and she had forgotten all about Bruno ... Then off Karl had gone again, on another multi-million-dollar deal, and it had been nights in a lonely bed thinking of him—trying *not* to think of him ... and the long hot days continued with the party to organise; the party—and Eleanora!

'My sweet child, of course there will be fireworks,' Eleanora had said. 'Is that not so, Carlo? Tell Laura there are always fireworks on these occasions ...' and Karl had looked up from his newspaper on this particular afternoon, and said that if there were always fireworks, then of course, they should have fireworks now. *If* it was what Laura wanted. He spoke in the cool voice reserved for the Contessa whenever she paid them her frequent visits, and it was the tone of his voice that kept Laura believing that nothing was going on between them now. But the glamorous Italian hadn't seemed to notice, and as she flirted with Karl on this particular occasion, Laura felt the old rage bursting inside. Karl should tell Eleanora to stay away. It wasn't right that he should subject Laura to his ex-mistress's presence. Yet who else was there to advise Laura?

'*Men*—they are all alike,' the Contessa said on another visit. 'They do not wish to become involved with the domestic affairs, but they expect even the newest of wives to run their homes with the smoothness of a

military campaign. It is not as if you were born into
such a household,' she added, with a specially consoling
smile that had made Laura grit her teeth.

Bruno's assistance was called for in the party plans;
alterations would have to be made to the drawing
and dining rooms. The terrace would be floodlit—and
how many extra staff would he require? And although
everything was only *suggested*, and Laura's approval
was needed in all things, eventually she felt like the
pig in the middle, superfluously bouncing about—not
really needed.

Karl brought the dressmaker back with him from
Milan. 'Look, I'm perfectly capable of going to Milan
and buying my own dress!' Laura wanted to scream. But
such things weren't done in the Rievenbeck household,
and when she muttered something far more mild on
the subject, Karl had looked vaguely surprised and
said didn't she realise how hot it was in Milan—
surely she didn't begrudge the dressmaker a few
relatively cool days in the mountains. So Laura had
bitten her cheek and let herself be caught up in the
vortex of an ancient aristocratic family, trying to
learn their ways, yet determined to keep her own
identity, her independence.

Replies to the invitations began pouring in only
days after she had sent them out. Many people would
be staying for the night, so there were all the extra
guest rooms to organise. As August drew to a close,
Laura's life seemed to revolve around one list or
another. Then there was a crisis with the caterers;
then the electricians didn't arrive until the day before
the party to decorate the terrace. Laura's dress
arrived in plenty of time, but it was too long, even if
she wore her highest heels, so back it had to go, and
Eleanora was furious—although what it had to do
with her, Laura couldn't imagine.

So the strange limbo period of adjustment gradually
slid into days of hectic activity. Sometimes Laura
managed to escape for a wander round the island, and

several times she met Tonio de Vito, who somehow always seemed to time his visits for when Karl was away. He had offered to take her sailing again, but she had refused, preferring not to encourage him; happy to sit and chat for a while, trying to find out if he had had any success with finding another racing boat.

He looked at her sideways, a thought suddenly striking him. 'You would like to buy me a boat?'

'Don't be silly,' she laughed.

'Why silly? You are wealthy. You could afford it.'

Could she? 'But I don't know you . . .' she began, still a bit flustered but trying to laugh it off. Was that why he had been coming here all this time? Did he seriously think . . .?

'I don't mean as a gift—I mean,' his sudden excitement momentarily deprived him of his English, 'as a—partnership. A business arrangement.'

'You mean like people have shares in racehorses?' Laura stammered.

'That is right.' Dark Latin eyes smiled encouragingly.

'I couldn't. I—don't have that kind of money. Karl wouldn't . . .'

'It is necessary to tell your husband?'

'Yes,' she said firmly, and Tonio saw at once that that was the end of that!

'It is a pity—it would have solved many things.' Then he tried to smile again. 'But if you should change your mind . . .'

'You'll be the first to know. I'd better go now—and so had you, it's a wonder you haven't been discovered.'

'But I have been,' he said, and when she frowned worriedly, he added, '*You* discovered me.'

'Idiot!' She laughed and threw a tiny pebble at him, racing off and calling back that she wouldn't come down here again if he was going to tease her. And he was still standing there, staring after her, as she reached the edge of the cove and scrambled up the rocks. He was a strange fellow. Likeable—but secretive. Did he really imagine she would part with so much money, or enter into a business partnership with a stranger? Getting a new boat and racing next season must mean a lot to him. Laura hoped he would find some other way to be successful.

But when she went back into the pre-party turmoil up at the villa she forgot all about Tonio and his boat. Her dress had come back, with only a day to spare, and it was fine this time and she smuggled it up to her room, so that no one would see it until the proper time. It was a gorgeous fairytale dress made of old patchwork lace. Eleanora had wanted her to have something more dramatic, classical, but Laura knew her young, slim figure and soft bouncing curls wouldn't have suited so severe a style.

The day before the party Eleanora moved in, Karl hadn't returned from Milan when she arrived and had installed herself in one of the best guest bedrooms overlooking the lake. 'You are looking tired, Laura,' she said, drawing her dark, beautifully shaped eyebrows together in apparent concern. 'You must have an early night. No excuses. We cannot have the bride looking jaded when the party is to be held in her honour. There is nothing now left to do that I cannot manage.' And she shooed Laura up to her room, where, truth to tell, she was only too glad to flop into bed. Almost instantly she was sound asleep.

Karl brought her supper up. She woke as he came into the room and quickly struggled on to her elbow. 'You shouldn't have. I'll come down,' but he placed the tray on the bedside table and smoothing himself a patch of bedclothes, he sat down.

'You are ill?' Blue eyes studied her face as his fingers gently brushed against her cheek.

'Of course not.' She clasped his hand and kissed it. 'How long have you been home? I didn't hear the launch.'

'Not long. You look pale.'

'Nonsense! I'm getting up.'

'No, Laura.' His voice was quiet, but firm. 'Undress and get properly into bed. Come.' He began undoing her blouse.

She kissed him.

'No.'

'Why not?' Her hands sneaked inside his lightweight summer jacket.

'Because you must rest.' He caught her hands and stilled them. 'Please, Laura—for me. Have your supper—then sleep,' and he helped—no, *forced*, her to undress as if she had been a child, and the lines of his face were cool and impassive for once.

'But we have guests,' Laura tried again.

'Eleanora does not consider herself a guest,' he said without thinking, and Laura pulled a face. 'If I say you need rest, that is what will happen. You have overtired yourself—unless . . .'

'Unless what?' she picked up quickly.

'Nothing.' He fetched her broderie anglaise negligée to slip round her bare shoulders while she sat up and ate her supper. 'Now, be good. Think of tomorrow. I shall be up presently and I shall expect to find you asleep. Promise?' He kissed her briefly, and although she wanted to cling on to him, something made her stop. She felt mixed up; pleased with his concern, unsure of his reasons. With Laura out of the way he could have a cosy little supper party with Eleanora.

He left her, and she scrambled out of bed and looked at herself in the mirror. She didn't look pale, just a bit tired perhaps. Not that she was going to interrupt them, she wouldn't give either of them the satisfaction of knowing how much she cared.

She climbed back into bed and pulled the tray of chicken salad and strudel across her knees. She was mad, out of her mind, to have worked herself silly organising this party, or rather, traipsing round saying, 'Yes, Eleanora—no, Eleanora,' bleating like some silly sheep. And tomorrow the house would be full of people she didn't know, because it hadn't occurred to anyone to invite Anthea or any of her friends, not that any of the girls could have afforded the fare from Paris. But Anthea would have come from Nice, or Venice, or wherever she was. *Any* familiar face would have been so comforting.

She couldn't finish the salad, managing instead only a few sips of wine and half the strudel. But her appetite had disappeared and without really choosing to do so, somehow she was snuggling down under the duvet and falling asleep.

Her appetite was still missing in the morning, in fact she was feeling decidedly queasy, but that was probably nerves about the party—and also because now she was suffering from the lack of food. So she struggled through breakfast and felt so amazingly better afterwards that she wasn't even daunted when the florist arrived with a launch-full of flowers ... the countdown to the party had begun.

Eleanora emerged from her room a little before midday, looking cool and elegant in a white pleated skirt and silk shirt in a multitude of blues and greens. A scarf of the same material wound her hair off her face, large dark glasses obscured her eyes and high spiky sandals click-clacked along the terrace as she discovered the shady spot where everyone was sipping a restorative gin and tonic.

'You shouldn't have let me sleep so long,' Eleanora began, and because of the sunglasses, Laura couldn't tell if she glanced at Karl as she spoke.

Laura gripped her glass and automatically replied to something the florist had just said to her. She was a pleasant girl, an American, doing mostly contract work for a large firm in Milan. Laura smiled and asked her how long she had been in Italy, and as she did she felt the knot of unease return to her stomach as Karl poured a drink for Eleanora and they both wandered over to the balustrade, with its magnificent backdrop of brilliant blue sky and white-topped mountains, their mirror image reflected in a shimmering lake.

The American girl followed Laura's eyes. 'Isn't this the most terrific place?' she drawled in her southern accent. 'I guess you'll never get used to it—take it for granted, I mean,' and Laura shook her head, hardly hearing, because she was desperately trying to hear what Karl and Eleanora were saying, as well as trying to remember what time Karl had come to bed. But she couldn't hear anything beyond the Contessa's brief charming laugh, and she couldn't remember when Karl had come to bed, except that once she had woken up and he hadn't been there—and the next time, he had. She watched, tortured, as the two lovers stood side by side, Eleanora's body swaying imperceptibly towards him, and Karl bending his head nearer, ostensibly to catch some secret whispered in his ear. They made a perfect picture, both expensively yet casually dressed. Eleanora a vision of blue, white and green; Karl in grey, close-fitting slacks and a superbly tailored shirt that exactly matched his eyes. Suddenly it was all too much.

'Do come and show me how you've transformed the drawing room,' she said to the florist. They went off together and Laura didn't give a backward glance. Suddenly she had made up her mind about something that she hadn't even wanted to think about. Tomorrow, after the party, there were going to be some changes made around here. It was up to Karl. He could choose. But either Eleanora went—or she did.

Strange how Laura felt better after that. Or was it because secretly she believed that Karl truly loved her? Uppermost in her mind she kept the knowledge that it was herself he had chosen when Eleanora had been perfectly free to marry. Wasn't that proof enough of his love?

So when the guests started arriving through the afternoon she could meet them with only a slight trepidation, because she was Laura Rievenbeck, the new bride, and there wouldn't have been a party if it hadn't been for her. Some friends came up from Milan, those were the people staying overnight; Karl had sent his little jet for them. But mostly they were people already up in the mountains for the summer.

The pace hotted up around teatime, when the musicians arrived and it was discovered that no one had considered they would need a meal. So Laura saw to it, while Karl showed the last of the overnight guests to their rooms; Eleanora had already disappeared to get ready.

Laura chatted to the musicians for quite a while, or rather they chatted in Italian and she more or less got the drift of what they were saying. Then she showed them the ground floor room where they could shower and change, and they kept asking her, teasing her, to sing with them. She realised it hadn't occurred to them that she was Karl's wife. Funny—she must still look like an art student. Why did everyone expect Laura Rievenbeck to look any different?

She escaped out of a side door near the kitchen quarters. She could hear Bruno lecturing his regiment of extra help and she had to pick her way carefully between crates of champagne. Shouldn't they already be on ice?

What a fuss! She wandered round to the terrace. It was after five o'clock but still pleasantly hot, with a little breeze coming off the water. Just right for a party tonight. She realised the fairy lights were switched on. Already? Then she saw an electrician with a basket of coloured bulbs, gradually replacing all those that had blown. So much to do—so many people involved for a few short hours of fun, put on especially for her . . . It made her feel strangely humble.

So she left him to it, there really wasn't anything more she could do, and feeling like a naughty child, she sneaked down the steps and along the jetty, sitting down on the slatted boards and dipping her toes in the water. No wonder the musicians thought she was a member of staff! And wouldn't she rather be out here, dangling her feet in the water, remembering other parties which had just meant putting on clean jeans and a pretty blouse and bringing a bottle of plonk; where the food had been chilli con carne or spaghetti bolognese, bubbling away in a tiny, steamy kitchen in giant saucepans, most of which were borrowed.

But all that had gone now. She sighed. And instead of London or the crowded back streets of Paris, here she was on a perfect island surrounded by incredible scenery, hearing the sad toll of church bells across the water. And instead of a tiny apartment, she lived in a beautiful hotchpotch of a house, almost a fortress, with the most wonderful man in the world.

'*And* a superb dress made of old lace,' she laughed to herself aloud, struggling up and slipping on her sandals. Then her face grew serious as she climbed the terrace steps. Cheese and plonk or champagne and lace dresses didn't really matter one way or the other. What mattered was Karl. Karl and their marriage together. And Laura knew she wasn't going to loose either without a fight.

CHAPTER EIGHT

'GET out—get *out*!' Laura threw a pillow at Karl. 'How
dare you come in here now! Have you any idea of the
time? Don't try and tell me you've been *talking* to our
guests until dawn!' She picked up another pillow and
hurled that one as well. 'Get out—go on! Sleep in your
own room. Isn't that what you really want?' Desperate,
angry beyond imagination, she looked round wildly for
something heavy and dangerous to throw at him. That
was it. It was all over now. Fight for him? Hah! Fight
with him, more like.

'Laura, have you gone out of your mind?' He looked
tired. *Tired*! Well, he would, wouldn't he? 'What is the
meaning of this behaviour? Do you want to wake the
whole house?'

'Don't you lecture me like some Victorian grand-
father!' she retaliated, grabbing the bedcover now, as if
it could possibly be a protection. '*I* know where you've
been. I *saw* you and Eleanora at the fireworks. Don't
try and deny it.' And in her mind's eye it was all vivid
and real again; the party was in full swing and everyone
was complimenting her on a wonderful success . . .

The house and terrace had been full of laughing,
chattering couples and Laura had drifted between them,
in a daze really, confident in her beautiful dress of creamy
lace, low-cut and off the shoulder, with Karl's pendant
of pearl and gold suspended above her cleavage. Her hair
had gone just right; it had grown longer lately and the
usually wayward curls had allowed themselves to be
brushed into just the right degree of casual orderliness.She
knew she had never looked as lovely. She seemed to have a
new glow about her, a glow that was noticed and had
drawn men to her side all evening. There had been
dancing out on the terrace under the little coloured

fairy lights, and the setting had been extra magical with the lights from the town reflected in the water, as if they had been putting on their own special show for her. So busy had she been as hostess that she had hardly seen Karl, equally busy as host. But at last, as she had gone to put a glass back on a table and was momentarily alone, he had suddenly been at her side, catching her arm above the elbow, and whispering, 'Let's get away from here.'

They had slipped, unseen, down the terrace steps and along to the waterfront. A cluster of launches were bobbing together down by the jetty, there were some giggles coming from one of them, so Karl took Laura's hand and led her down a little secret path, heavy with the scent of night flowers. They passed beneath a large, concealing shrub, and tenderly, so tenderly, Karl had taken her in his arms and started kissing her.

'You are the most beautiful woman here tonight, do you know that?' he had murmured, his hands sliding up and down her spine until her whole back tingled.

She sighed in contentment, wanting to believe him, needing this reassurance; needing the familiar, but always to be wondered at, spell he could cast over her ... His lips left her own and dragged across her cheek, down to her throat; he was nibbling at her, tasting her—wanting to eat her.

She slipped her hands inside his white jacket and pressed herself against the long, hard, intoxicated length of him. 'It's a lovely party,' she whispered. 'Thank you.'

He eased her from him. 'I wish everyone would disappear.' And now his hands smoothed her bottom and thighs through the thin lacy material and they both groaned softly as their hips swayed together. 'Where can we go?' he breathed urgently, and she felt the familiar tension straining at his body.

'We mustn't.'

'Why not?'

'Because ...' There were voices above them on the terrace ...

'It's all right, they can't see us down here.' And because she was still uncertain, he began kissing her again, undoing her zip, so that the off-the-shoulder dress began sliding down her arms.

'Karl!' It was a mixture of laughter, confusion and retribution as she tried to remain respectable.

'No—let me see you,' and his taunting, magical lips blazed a delicate white-hot trail across her shoulder, down her arm, before capturing her full, red-tipped breast as it began peeping over her dress.

'Someone might come. Oh . . .' It was exquisite.

'No one will come.' His voice was deep and husky with desire.

'Karl, darling . . .' She squeezed her eyes tight shut with the agony of it. 'I can't bear it—it isn't fair!'

'The boathouse,' he said quickly. 'Come——'

'Don't be silly.' She struggled to hitch up her dress. Heavens, if anyone should come now!

'I don't mean the launch.' His night eyes flashed dangerously. 'The cruiser—my cabin—*quickly!*'

She swayed against him, wanting him, loving him, her body responsive and ready. 'Do me up first . . .' Oh, this was crazy, surely the host and hostess shouldn't disappear to make love in a boat while the party went on without them!

Then suddenly the music on the terrace had stopped and someone was calling for Karl.

'Take no notice,' he whispered urgently. 'Come . . .' but Laura hung back, recognising the voice.

'Car-lo . . .!' It was Eleanora, and then she began calling out in Italian and he cursed and sighed, and squeezed Laura's arm.

'They want to start the fireworks; it must be midnight.'

Laura swallowed. 'Oh dear!'

'I'm sorry, darling. We—should really go.'

'You go—I'll—I'll come in a minute,' and although he had protested, Laura had stayed behind down in the darkened garden, straightening her dress, calming her

body, tidying her hair. She was just about to go back up
when the terrace lights went out and everything was
plunged into blackness. So she stayed where she was,
watching the sky, and then it began; gold, silver, reds
and greens—rockets and shooting stars—golden rain.
And there were 'oohs' and 'ahhs' just like the children.
Really it was quite bright; she made her way easily to
the bottom of the steps. Then another lot of fireworks
shot off and burst into the night sky, hanging there,
showers of gold and silver making everything as bright
as day. Several people applauded and Laura glanced up
at everyone, looking almost ghostly in the monochrome
light. And they were all staring upwards ... except two
people at the back of the terrace, two people who
seemed more interested in each other. The eerie light
held for several seconds longer, long enough for Laura
to have recognised Karl and Eleanora. And Karl had
been leaning towards her—*kissing* her ...

The party—the whole evening—everything had been
ruined. Laura had picked up her skirts and had hurried
back down into the garden. That was it. That told her
everything. Eleanora had tried to warn her—well, she
wouldn't need any more evidence. Karl was still having
an affair with his mistress; without knowing it, he had
already made his choice.

And now, as Laura sat up in bed clutching the
bedcover, and frantically searching for something else
to throw at him, she wondered at his nerve for daring to
stay with that woman all night, and actually coming to
his wife's bed afterwards at five o'clock in the morning.

Karl had caught the pillows and now he threw them
on to a chair. 'You're overtired,' he said, 'you don't
know what you're saying.'

'I know perfectly well what I'm saying.' Green eyes
flashed dangerously. 'I'm saying get out of here. Sleep
in your own room!'

'Very well.' The strong lines of his face were drawn in
masculine aggression. 'I thought you went to bed
because you were feeling tired again, but I see I was

mistaken.' He took off his jacket as he spoke and threw it over another chair. Laura hardly noticed.

'Is that what you told our guests? How convenient! Well, I wasn't tired, not a bit. I just refused to stay down there at that, that—*charade*. Is that why you took me down into the garden? The trouble is, I didn't stay down there long enough. I saw you afterwards, on the terrace with Eleanora. You were *kissing* her. Anyone could have seen. How *dare* you bring her here! How *dare* you insult me. How dare you sleep with her and expect to share this bed!'

Karl ripped off his bow tie, tossed it on the floor and began undoing his shirt. 'Do not accuse me of having an affair when my wife is under the same roof! Many things I have done in my life—but never that.' The shirt came off, he screwed it into a ball and flung it away.

'You haven't had the opportunity up till now, have you?' Laura shouted back, her blonde curls dancing about angrily. 'Don't think I've been fooled because you're always so cool and remote with her—*when I'm about*. But how many times do you meet her when you're supposed to be away on business? Right from the beginning it was always her, wasn't it? In Paris, when you left on that first trip and phoned me from Rome—I heard a woman's voice. It was *her*, wasn't it? Answer me! Even then, having just proposed to me, you went straight to Eleanora Ferrara!'

'For once you are perfectly correct, my dear Laura,' and how fractured his accent sounded, as if he was having great difficulty remembering his English. He kicked off his shoes and his hand went to the belt of his trousers.

'What—are you doing?' Laura stammered, at last realising what he was doing.

'I am coming to bed.'

'I *said* you're sleeping in your own room—you're not spending what's left of this night with me, Karl Rievenbeck!'

'You have made that perfectly clear.' He undressed

completely before her startled eyes, and now he was
standing there tall and proud, aggressive, naked,
deadly. 'But we began something earlier, something
which I have been waiting all night to complete.'

'No.'

He moved like lightning. 'Yes, Laura. This minute. I
have waited long enough.' He caught her as she tried to
scramble out of bed.

'Then you'll have to go and see what Eleanora can do
for you—again,' she added insultingly. And, oh dear, he
was going to hit her, she could feel the rage beating out
of him as their arms and legs tangled together.

'I do not want Eleanora—I want you. I am your
husband, Laura. Your *husband*. It's time you began to
realise what that means.' He was pushing her back into
the pillows, his weight trapping her, excitement and
desire darkening the anger in his eyes.

Heavens, what would he do to her? Laura squirmed
and fought, remembering the last time they had done
so, when she had bitten him—and sudden remorse had
made everything all right, and in the end he had been
passionate but tender. Yet nothing like that was
happening now, because it was too late for tenderness
of any kind. She had caught him out. She now knew he
was being unfaithful and there was no reason for him to
pretend to love Laura. This was just sex, lust, the
aggressive male ego making another conquest.

'Get off—I hate you!' but it was useless, useless, and
through it all her damned body was responding to him
in spite of everything. She was fighting, kicking,
punching, but every time she made contact with the
magnificent hardness of his body, every time they rolled
over and over and her senses were filled with the
arousing male scent of him, it began—inside her; the
needing, the wanting, so that when she finally struck a
blow across his face, he roared and took her in a storm
of passion that even now couldn't be called rape.

'Beast! Swine!' she yelled, arching her back, trying to
thrust him off. 'Oh, God!' She clenched her fists and

squeezed her eyes tight shut in fury. Why did it have to be so exciting, so stimulating? Why, even now, could he drive her wild? . . .

She had been right. There was no tenderness, no caressing, no waiting for her. Karl used her. He used her body to give him sexual satisfaction, which was all he could have hoped for that night. And she wanted to hate him—tomorrow she would. It began . . . and she fought it. No, it wasn't going to happen. She wasn't special any more. She would stop it. 'Go *away*!' she cried out desperately, as deep waves of sensation began throbbing inside her, and he knew—lord, he *knew* what she really meant, and with a cry of triumph he drove her remorselessly, thunderingly, through the barrier of this world—and into oblivion.

He was there as a dim, misty figure as she opened her eyes, gasping, frightened—not sure where she was. She even imagined he said, 'Ssh—you're all right, *liebling* . . .' and she had clung to him and cried . . . And then sleep had come for a few, drifting minutes, and he had still been there—and the world wasn't real.

But now he was moving, rolling away from her, and she opened her eyes, drugged heavy with love. 'Where are you going?' she whispered.

'To my room,' and the sharp diction cut through the memory of their passion.

'What do you mean?' Still rather confused, Laura struggled up on one elbow.

He threw the duvet over her and she noticed the cool hardness of those blue eyes. 'You told me to sleep in my own room—and from now on I shall. But don't think that will make any difference to my access to your body. You are my wife. It is my right. I have just demonstrated what will happen whenever I want you. You will not be able to change things. Any time of the day or night—here, or wherever we happen to be. I will not be dissuaded by either your rage or your tears. You are *my wife*,' he repeated, his normally sexy accent cutting the air like a knife. 'But I agree not to sleep with you again. Sleeping with someone requires trust—which you have yet to learn.' He made an attempt to pick up his scattered clothes as he walked purposefully towards the door. 'When you are ready to talk like an adult—when you wish to sleep with me again—come to my bed. Until then I will not disturb you.'

'Except when taking what you imagine is your right,' Laura muttered through tight, trembling lips.

'Precisely.' Karl gave a brief, acknowledging nod. 'Except when taking what I *know* is my right.'

His *right*! His *right*! Alone again, Laura sank back into the pillows and bit back the tears. You could even say it was his *divine* right. Damn him! Curse him. Why, even now, *especially* now, did she know she needed and loved Karl Rievenbeck, if not as much as, then probably *more* than ever? Oh, what a hopeless mess!

The last of the overnight guests left in the launch after lunch, or more properly, after a buffet breakfast that had begun at ten and gone on until midday. All of the guests except Eleanora, of course, who actually came down to the jetty with Karl and Laura to wave them off. It was hot again today, but oppressive, and the gathering clouds might be heralding a storm.

'I think everyone enjoyed themselves,' said Karl in a withdrawn preoccupied voice, to which Eleanora quickly responded.

'Of course they did, *cara*,' she gleamed, slipping her arm into his and leaning into him. 'It was a superb affair—the best I've—we've arranged.'

'I'm sure Laura appreciated your help,' he said, drawing away to pick off the dead-head of a flower in one of the colourful tubs.

They had reached the terrace steps, and Laura hung back, not wanting to be part of this trio, wishing the Contessa anywhere but here, hating Karl for letting her stay; so right at this moment she couldn't have thanked Eleanora for her help—it would have choked her.

The silence stretched into a little eternity; Karl's face was grim, he would expect politeness whatever the circumstances. 'Eleanora,' he began after a moment, 'I wonder if I might speak with you in my study—er—those investments you wanted me to organise ...' He glanced back at Laura, his eyes blank, unfathomable. 'You will excuse us?' he added quietly.

No, no, *no*, she wouldn't. Their eyes locked, held, and she opened her mouth to protest; to hell with official propriety. But she was pre-empted by Bruno, who called down to them that there was a telephone call for Karl from London, so instead the two women were left alone, and Laura took a deep breath.

'I'd like to have a word with you myself,' she said, amazed that her voice sounded so steady. 'Shall we sit on the terrace, or would you prefer to go for a walk?'

Eleanora laughed. 'So serious!' Then her dark eyes were suddenly wary. 'We sit, I think. After last night I need a little rest.'

I bet you do, Laura wanted to say. But now wasn't the time—not yet.

'Karl—is right,' Laura began, as they settled themselves on padded garden chairs. 'I do appreciate the help you've given me with the party; I wouldn't have known where to begin ...' A man on steps was taking down the fairy lights, she hoped he didn't understand English.

'It was a pleasure, my dear Laura. I do not remember when I have enjoyed myself more.'

'But I think you'd better know that I saw you last night,' Laura interrupted, before her nerve went. 'You and Karl, up here, during the firework display.'

The Contessa didn't pretend to misunderstand. 'So that's why we have so many gloomy faces this morning,' she said, unable to keep rich amusement out of her voice.

'I really don't see anything funny in the situation,' Laura replied.

The older woman's face darkened. 'And you have spoken to Carlo about this?'

'Yes.'

'That was a mistake,' said Eleanora.

'I think not.' Laura wound the tie belt of her dress into a tight roll. 'You lied to me,' and when the Contessa looked startled, she added, 'When you said you had no intention of waiting for Karl to come back to you. You had every intention, in fact, you planned that your affair with him should hardly be interrupted. And you actually expect me to sit back and watch it happen—and say *nothing*—*do* nothing, just to keep on living here?'

'You would be a fool to throw all this away,' the Contessa said derisively.

'Then you don't deny it?' It took a great deal of effort to appear outwardly calm, but inside Laura was trembling with the fear of what she was likely to learn now that she had started questioning.

'You are overwrought,' Eleanora began, smiling placatingly, her dark, voluptuous Roman eyes suddenly reminding Laura of someone. 'A kiss between ex-lovers . . .' But then she saw that Laura didn't believe her, and after a slight pause, she shrugged and smiled a slow, secret, nasty sort of smile, then leant comfortably back in her chair, crossing one elegant leg over the other. 'What else did you really expect?' she went on in a different, harder voice, that Laura hadn't heard before. 'You have seen Carlo's friends. You have seen the people he mixes with; bankers, politicians, foreign officials. Men of intelligence, taste, discrimination . . .' She could have been describing Karl Rievenbeck himself; the words had a deadly truth about them. 'You have seen the women who accompany such men. Women who were born into such worlds. Carlo needs me. He will always need me. His marriage to you only adds to that need—it does not decrease it.'

Laura dug her fingernails into the palm of her hand until she almost shouted out in agony. 'So why didn't

he marry *you*?' she said, sensing now that she would get
the real answer to her question. 'If he can't do without
you, why aren't *you* the new Rievenbeck bride? Why, if
he loves you so much, did he cast you aside after a ten-
year affair, the moment you were suddenly free to
marry him?' As she spoke she watched every move on
the Contessa's face. Her reaction was vital. If there was
any jealousy, any anger at such abandonment, now was
the moment for it to appear. But there was none.
Instead, Eleanora smiled in bright amusement, almost
laughing that Laura should come to such a foolish
conclusion.

'My dear Laura, you do not imagine that Carlo—
that he *abandoned* me! Such an idea is preposterous.
I'm sorry,' which she obviously wasn't, 'I thought it
was common knowledge, naturally I assumed that
you knew . . .'

'Knew what?' Laura prompted, in case she should slide
into secrecy again.

'Knew that my husband made it impossible for me to
marry again,' she said, and now there was a touch of
bitterness in her words that rang absolutely true. 'He was
a very wealthy man, *very* wealthy,' she continued, 'and
most of his estate comes to me, *if* I don't remarry. If I
do,' she shrugged, 'then everything goes to the children
of his former marriage, who are all grown up with
fortunes of their own and can hardly need any more.'

'So you mean Karl waited, asked you—to marry
him,' Laura managed to say.

'But of course.' Dark eyes widened in surprise. 'But
how was it possible? It would have meant me losing so
much . . .'

Laura waved her hands around. 'What about all this?
Doesn't he have more than enough for both of you?'

'When you reach my age—with my experience,' said
Eleanora, 'you will value the importance of financial
independence. I do not give that up for nobody,' she
added, her grammar failing her—but her meaning
perfectly clear.

And suddenly everything was clear to Laura as well. Karl had been in love with this woman, and had wanted to marry her. How did a man like Karl Rievenbeck react to such a blow to his pride? By marrying the first woman who came along? As a means of hitting out at Eleanora, or simply to continue the Rievenbeck line? Had they really planned it together, as she had suspected? Look how quickly he had returned to her in Rome after their hasty engagement.

There were voices suddenly from inside, Karl and Bruno talking about an unexpected trip to London, but Laura knew she couldn't face her husband yet. She was deeply hurt, confused, unsure where to go from here.

'Tell him I've gone for a walk,' she said, jumping up and running around the end of the terrace before he saw her. Eleanora hadn't replied, instead her eyes had glowed with malicious triumph, and Laura had cursed herself for ever believing the Contessa had wanted to be a friend.

It was so hot. She escaped by clambering down the rocks at the side of the house, and away from the ornamental gardens to the little beach where she had met Tonio. No one else ever came here; she took off her sandals and paddled along the waterline, feeling as low and heavy as the clouds rumbling in and obscuring the mountain-tops. What was she going to do? How could you live with a man, loving him desperately, but knowing he had married you for all the wrong reasons?

She went for a swim, slipping off her creamy shirtwaister dress and plunging into the flat, grey water in her lacy white bra and pants; they became instantly transparent, which Laura would have found amusing in the normal way—but not today. She swam back and forth, being careful to keep within her depth; silly to be so nervous. Then she floated, but decided she was beginning to feel chilly. And swimming hadn't solved her problems either. So she waded out, just happening to glance back over her shoulder, and—oh, no, there was the little dinghy with the blue and white sails!

Tonio was the last person she wanted to meet right
now. So she hurried back into her dress, which stuck to
her in all the wrong places, but she was past caring
now.

Then she hurried out of sight, cross at the
interruption, knowing she didn't want to go back to the
house. And then she remembered the boat-house, and
suddenly the idea of being alone and free seemed an
excellent idea.

'I want to take out a *boat*,' Laura repeated,
exasperatedly in English. *'Boat.'* She waved her hands.
'Out on the lake,' and the boatman nodded and smiled,
then went off in a volley of German which ended up by
sounding as if the taking out of boats was strictly
forbidden.

Laura marched out in a huff. There was only one
person who could issue such orders—Karl. She hadn't
been off this island for practically six weeks! If she
didn't get away soon she would scream. *Scream!*
Shivering, she stared up at the house, its roof etched
high and uneven against the darkening sky. For a
moment it looked like a castle—like Dracula's castle,
with its turrets and tower, and high, inaccessible
windows . . . Why did Karl want to persist with this
sham of a marriage? Much better to let her leave. And
suddenly everything closed in on her, and she ran away,
back to the beach, racing through the undergrowth,
twigs and branches tugging at her dress and hair . . .
She broke cover and ran out on to the beach—and
there was Tonio, in shorts and tee-shirt, looking dark
and handsome and smiling at the unexpected sight of
her as if she had made his day.

'You shouldn't be here—one day you'll be caught!'
Laura shouted at him. Then she wasn't standing still
any more, but was running towards him, throwing her
arms around him—and the tears began to fall.

'Take me away,' she sobbed, against his chest. The
words had spoken themselves; if they surprised her,
they left Tonio absolutely speechless. 'Take me far—far

away. Now, this minute!' she added fiercely, pulling
back and staring up at him, *willing* him to do as she
asked.

'But,' he swallowed, 'your husband . . .'

'*You're* not frightened of him as well?' she snorted,
remembering the man in the boat-house.

His face darkened, his masculinity threatened, yet
caution tempered his reply. 'You are upset,' he began
carefully, his hand smoothing her arm. 'It is not right
for you to do anything hasty. Sit down over here,' and
he led her over to a rock, fetching his sweater from the
boat when she started to shiver, and offering her his
hanky. 'What would people say if they saw you—
dressed with only . . .' he meant, 'with only the clothes
you stand up in,' but he couldn't find the right
translation, 'they will say I have napkidded you.'

'Kidnapped,' Laura corrected, without even a hint of
a smile on her face.

'So—kidnapped. Do you not agree? You have no
luggage—such things must be considered.'

Laura sniffed. 'I thought that's why you've been
coming here,' she said. 'I thought you wanted to
persuade me to go away with you.'

He looked uncomfortable. 'Yes.' She wasn't surprised.
'But——'

'But?' she prompted.

'You have not seemed—very keen to get to know
me.' Tonio wasn't looking at her any more; the end of
the headland held a sudden fascination for him.

'You haven't tried to make me—keen.' Why was she
doing this, testing him? She must be out of her mind!

He looked at her sideways, suspiciously. Why
suspiciously? 'Who have you been talking to?' he said.

'Talking?' Laura frowned. 'I don't know what you
mean. Don't you *want* to take me away?' she asked,
doing a third-rate impression of a coquette for the first
time in her life.

'If that's what you really want.' Tonio didn't seem
exactly excited with the idea.

Laura looked down at her lap, feeling ashamed, confused . . . 'I don't know what I want,' she whispered. 'I only know I want you to come back again—tomorrow. You will, won't you?' She clutched at his arm. 'Please say you'll come again. I have to have *someone*.' For a moment she almost laughed; even Anthea would be better than no one, right now.

'Of course I will come tomorrow.' He looked relieved, yet—bitter? 'If the weather makes it possible,' he reminded her, putting his arm around her shoulders and giving her a hug. 'You know, you are a very lovely woman,' he said seriously. 'I think your husband must be a little crazy in the head.'

'How did you know . . .' but she didn't add, 'that Karl doesn't love me,' because presumably that was the only reason that a new bride should be in such distress.

For a moment he looked awkward, embarrassed, then he suggested they went for a walk, to cheer her up, so they wandered down to the other end of the island where the ruined castle bore witness to time and a violent devastation.

'You have heard about the notorious Rievenbeck brothers?' Tonio asked, 'who lived here in the—er—*quattrocento*?'

'Fifteenth century?' Laura offered.

'*Si*—yes, there were five of them.'

'Five?' she interrupted, appalled at the idea of five dominant men like Karl.

Tonio nodded. 'And it was said that no woman was safe from one end of the lake to the other. Married or virgins, they would be brought here to this island fortress, where escape was impossible.'

Laura looked up at the eyeless ruin and shivered, glad that Tonio was with her; for a moment identifying with those unfortunate women. No wonder Karl hadn't said anything when he had brought her here! 'What happened to them—afterwards?'

Tonio looked glum. 'It is better not to think. But the brothers—they were destroyed. In the end the people sent a private army. An army,' he repeated, 'to blast them out. But it took six months; the five brothers held out up there . . .' and he trailed to silence as they both visualised the bloody mediaeval scene.

'But they obviously didn't die out without establishing heirs,' said Laura, turning away, not wanting to stay . . .

Tonio helped her over some rough rocks as they began to make their way back to the beach. 'That was many years ago—you must not believe that your husband is such a man.'

'How would you know?' she snapped. Oh, how these men always stuck together! Then she was contrite at her impatience. It must have been a shock for him to have a married woman fling herself into his arms, especially when that woman was Karl Rievenbeck's wife! When they reached the beach, he picked up a stick and she watched him trace patterns in the wet shingle. His classical Roman profile accentuated high cheekbones, full lips and long curly lashes that fate ought to have bequeathed to a woman. What was he *really* doing here?

'You will come again tomorrow, won't you?' she asked, and he turned his head, the stick hanging limply in his hand, and his gorgeous eyes were dark and serious.

'If that is what you really want,' he said quietly.

Laura's glance slid away, and then she squeezed her eyes tight shut, trying to set her muddled thoughts in order. 'I need to know you'll come back—*should* I want to get away . . .'

'No problem.' He suddenly put his arm around her and kissed her quickly on the cheek. 'It is a great pity that you became involved in all this.' Then almost looking as if he had said too much, he suddenly realised it was almost five o'clock and he had an appointment to see a boat at the other end of the lake.

'A boat? You mean—for racing? You've found one?' For a moment she was delighted for him.

He pulled a face and gave a heavy shrug. 'Nothing is yet decided; it is still a question of the money.'

There wasn't an answer to that, so she helped him push the dinghy back into the water, just remembering in time to give him back his sweater as he raised the sail and made it fast.

Then they both heard the sound of a boat coming round the headland—oh no, it was the launch, going over to the town jetty. But it never usually came this way ... Whoever was on board would easily see everything on the beach. Maybe it was Karl. But as the boat suddenly came into sight Laura recognised Eleanora standing in the bows, her dark head covered by the blue and green headscarf she had worn the other day.

'Get down, get down!' Laura hissed, ducking behind the dinghy. 'It's the Contessa—if she sees you ...'

Tonio laughed. 'She will not know who it is from this distance. You should not worry. Come, give me a push,' and Laura reluctantly waded out, nearly up to her knees, and helped to twist the dingy round. He was probably right—yet if Karl should find out ...

'See you tomorrow, if the weather is not too bad,' Tonio called, waving and blowing her a kiss, and bringing the dinghy round to a close-haul and heading out of the little bay quite speedily. She hadn't noticed the wind get up. The launch had turned towards the mainland now, it was getting smaller and smaller ...

There was a distant rumble of thunder. Good, perhaps a storm would clear the air.

Laura stood watching the little dinghy gradually disappear, waving until she couldn't distinguish Tonio any more, then finally sighing and deciding she had better be going. Now, where had she put her sandals?

'Are these what you're looking for?' called an unexpected voice, and she gasped, stifling a scream, as a tall, familiar figure stepped out of the shadow of an overhanging rock. It was Karl.

'You—startled me! I didn't see you,' she stammered, swallowing and clutching the open neck of her dress. 'I went for a swim—it was so hot.' How long had he been there? What had he seen? What had he heard? 'I think there's going to be a storm,' she squeaked, and although her fear was perfectly evident, the displeasure on his face didn't relent, as he came across the gravelly beach to meet her. His long strides drew him remorselessly nearer—the lean hips and broad athletic frame marking him a man to be reckoned with.

He stopped, only a few paces in front of her, dangling the sandals like bait, but she was frightened of what would happen if she took them. At last she reached for them, but—yes, it was a mistake. A dangerous light flashed in his eyes and he caught her wrist, trapping her in an iron grip.

'Who was he? The man in the yacht? You were waving goodbye to him.' A sudden gust of wind blew the smooth dark hair across his forehead; he scraped it back with impatient fingers. 'Tell me, Laura!' He shook her. 'Who was that man? How many times have you met him? Have you arranged to see him again.' Now his face was livid with anger. 'Come—why are you silent? I demand an answer—*now*!'

CHAPTER NINE

'DEMAND all you like,' Laura retorted, 'but I can't give you an answer.' She broke free at last and took a couple of steps backwards. 'I can't help it if strangers decide to land here,' which was more or less the truth, because she didn't really know who Tonio was, did she?

'But the island is private—they should read the notices,' Karl growled. 'You should have told him so—you are my wife, Laura, and I expect . . .'

'Oh, we all *expect*, don't we?' she interrupted. 'I expected you to have married me because you loved me, not as some retribution—some evil dig at Eleanora because she wouldn't marry you.'

'What are you talking about? What has she told you?'

'Don't try and deny it—I know,' she retaliated, her blonde curls tossing about angrily. 'It must have been a shock, I'm sure; the great Karl Rievenbeck turned down because the grand Contessa would rather keep her money. Is that why you let her keep coming here? To show her what she's missing—what marriage to you would have been like?'

There was a thin white line around his lips. 'I allowed Eleanora to keep coming because I was under the impression that you needed her help with last night's party.'

'Of course I needed help—a little inexperienced nobody like me,' Laura snapped, remembering Eleanora's scathing remarks. 'But it didn't work, did it? You couldn't keep your hands off her. Ten years of sharing the same bed had become too much of a habit.'

'You are mistaken.'

'Like hell I am!' She turned away and marched

130

back along the beach.

Karl was right behind her. 'Eleanora has gone,' he said, catching Laura's arm and swinging her round so that she bumped into the solid wall of his chest. 'I have sent her away.'

'Oh—great! That's supposed to make a difference, is it?' She struggled away from him again, aware of the dark storm clouds gathering and another distant rumble of thunder. 'But we all know Eleanora's summer villa is only half an hour's drive away from here—I suppose *everyone* knows what's going on between the pair of you. Well, now I'm as wise as any of them—now I know why you really married me—and I've had enough!'

'What do you mean?' Each word was crisp, precise; like gunfire.

'I would have thought that was obvious.'

He swallowed. 'You are overtired. We'll talk about it when I get back from London.'

'Well, don't expect to find me here when you get back!' she almost shouted. Oh, this wasn't really happening, was it? But what alternative was there? It would only be a life of misery if she stayed.

'You don't know what you're saying.' He grabbed her arm again, desperate anger beating out of him, his eyes a violent blue. 'You are my wife—for better or worse, and you do *not* run out on me the first time things do not appear to go your own way.'

'You married me under false pretences, so vows don't count.' Laura squirmed in his arms, but he wasn't letting go this time. 'How long was it, tell me,' she insisted, 'how long after Eleanora told you she wouldn't marry you—how long between that and meeting me in Paris?'

A muscle jerked in his cheek.

'How long?' she shouted.

'About four weeks.'

'Four weeks!' Less than a month. Wide green eyes registered even more shock. 'You mean up to four weeks before meeting me you were planning to marry Eleanora?'

'Yes.' Then he took a long, steadying sigh, and his voice was a little less severe, as he added, 'But I didn't marry her—I married you.'

'You didn't have much option, did you? Couldn't get yourself a son quick enough, could you? Oh, I know all about you Rievenbecks.' She nearly added, 'Tonio told me,' but stopped herself just in time. 'That was your duty; to perpetuate the line. Find the first reasonable woman, preferably someone alone, someone dependable . . .' her voice nearly broke and she turned it into a cough. Oh, how everything all fitted together. His whirlwind romance, his choosing a young, vulnerable, as he thought *acquiescent* foreign girl, who would be isolated not only by youth and position, but also by the language barrier! How easy to keep such a girl a virtual prisoner on an island such as this. Shut off, dependent, willing or *forced* to turn a blind eye to his sexual intrigues for the sake of security—for the sake of her children. 'But it didn't work,' she continued aloud, 'because I'm not pregnant. And I'm not going to be incarcerated on this island while you go lording it all over the world. I don't give a damn about the Rievenbeck family name. I'm leaving you, Karl, and there's nothing you can do about it.'

He laughed. He actually laughed, if such a hoarse, rasping sound was worthy of the name. 'You will never leave me. If you did, do you think I would rest until I had found you?' and there was such menace in his voice that Laura was really frightened. It had taken an army to deal with the mediaeval Rievenbecks—so how could just one girl withstand the new, super, twentieth-century version? A man like Karl could make anything happen just by signing a cheque.

'Go away—leave me alone!' She shivered, missing Tonio's sweater. The wind was coming in gusts now, her dress still felt damp. She shivered again. 'Go on, leave me alone. Your money might have bought my body, but you'll never see into my mind—never!'

Karl looked as if he was going to hit her. Then all the rage, all the violence drained out of him and his face was a blank, enigmatic mask. And there was no emotion in his actions as he reached out, fingering the open neck of her dress, running a proprietorial yet disinterested hand down the buttons—undoing them . . . His cold blue eyes hard and brittle as he exposed soft, full breasts straining against the damp nylon of her bra. But there was no desire in his eyes, no pleasure, and when he spoke it was in the hard tone of a business man.

'As much as I want a son—as much as you acknowledge my right to your body—I trust you will forgive me for not taking advantage of the offer at this moment. I find the prospect does not seem to attract me.'

'Go away!' Laura broke the mesmerising hold of his eyes as she pulled her dress together. If he didn't leave in a minute she would break down in front of him. 'Just go away. Go to London. Stay there for all I care!' And that did it. At last he strode away, his shoes scrunching the shingle as she watched him go, her heart breaking, her face rigid. At last he had clambered over the rocks and was finally out of sight, and then she collapsed into a little heap and the tears finally came.

She caught a cold, a silly, stupid cold, with a temperature, that had her trapped in bed with everyone flapping about bringing her meals and hot drinks, so she couldn't run away for a few days yet—could she? Gradually the piles of thank-you letters began arriving, some in German, some in Italian, but at least the reading of them was good practice for her. Karl had gone to London. Why, he didn't say. Probably thought she wasn't intelligent enough to understand his business deals. Not that she cared . . .

Laura delved into the box of tissues again, plumped the pillows, determined not to give herself up to misery. The storm had blown itself out, but the weather was unsettled now—sunny one moment, cloudy with the threat of rain, the next.

Had Tonio come back to the beach? There was no way of knowing, no way of letting him know what had happened to her. Had he seen Karl on the beach? Would he be scared for her—or scared for himself? She wondered if he had managed to buy the powerboat— how long would his holiday last?

On the third day she got up, her temperature had gone, some fresh air would do her good. So she stretched out on a lounger in the warm September sunshine, pretending to read, but really trying to decide what she was going to do—and how she was going to get away from here if Tonio didn't come back.

There was a message from Karl to say he would be back the following day. Which meant that if she was going to do anything it had to be during the next twelve hours. There were several boats out on the lake and she kept her eyes open for one with blue and white sails . . . perhaps he would come after lunch. If he could put her on a bus, maybe . . . tell her where the nearest railway station was. She could get back to Paris, back to Colette's flat. The idea of going to Nice and asking for Anthea's support was too silly to contemplate seriously. Or was Anthea already in Venice?

'Do you think the world is large enough for you to hide?' Karl's words continually returned to terrify her. Could he drag her back here wherever she went? Would he really want to live with a wife who refused to conform to his specification of the role?

But oh, she didn't want to go. She leaned back in her lounger, agony tearing at her soul, knowing she would love Karl for ever. Could she find the strength to go on living with him even though he had another woman? Would that torment be slightly less than the torment of never seeing him again?

She screwed up her eyes to shut the tears in; the September sunshine mocking her in a patch of sudden summer brightness. September? *September!* Her eyes flew open and she sat bolt upright. That meant August was over; the last *week* in August. And ... But she had got it wrong. So she raced up to her room and grabbed the diary out of her bag. One, two, three—four and a half weeks ... That meant she was ten days overdue. With all the work for the party she just hadn't given it a thought ...

She sat down on the bed quickly, wide-eyed, suddenly breathless, grinning, feeling excited yet at the same time telling herself that it was really too soon to be sure. But she had never been even a day late. So she just sat there on the edge of the bed, staring out of the French windows, her brain all cottonwool, her body all sensations, as she actually contemplated the serious possibility that she was pregnant.

What would Karl say? *What would Karl say!* Like a cold douche reality came tumbling back. Now he would have what he wanted. And if the baby was a boy he wouldn't even have to go through the pretence of loving her, because then she would be committed to staying here for ever. What mother could deny her child such a home; such an inheritance?

But were money and position everything? What life would it be for the child living with the tension of opposing parents? And Karl would probably send him away to school—and she would be so lonely here ...

It was decision time, and feeling restless, Laura skipped lunch and wandered down to the beach, but there was still no sign of Tonio. No sign of the little dinghy anywhere on the lake, and she didn't know whether to be pleased or sorry. She wanted to talk with him again, wanted to discover if he really would take her away ... And yet what a relief not to have to make a decision just at this moment.

The launch was heading ashore as Laura made her way back to the house. How easily the servants moved about, compared to herself. Or had it gone to fetch someone? Was Karl back? So she hurried to his study and found the binoculars ... Yes, it was coming back—

only from this distance it would be impossible to distinguish the passenger.

Puzzled, somehow certain it wasn't Karl, she ran down to the jetty just as the launch came alongside, and she took the bowline and slipped the loop over a bollard. There was a movement in the cabin, cases were being carried out; blue cases, she didn't recognise them, and then a woman was speaking in English, telling them to be careful with something, and Laura took a couple of steps backwards, as she suddenly recognised the voice.

'Darling, there you are! I'm so glad you're back. They said you'd gone for a walk when I phoned.' It was all Laura could do not to stand there with her mouth open. What was *Anthea*, of all people, doing here?

'What a lovely surprise,' she managed to say, helping her stepmother ashore. Anthea looked very well, very stylish, her red hair crisply swept up, her cream linen two-piece trim and uncrumpled. High spiky shoes and matching bag were in her favourite snakeskin. She didn't look as if she had travelled far. 'Have you—have you come from Nice?' Laura added, 'or Venice?'

'Don't talk to me about Nice; it was dreadful,' said Anthea, taking Laura's arm as if they had been good friends for years. But her eyes were everywhere, taking in the magnificent house, towering over them, the terraced gardens, a riot of flowers. She saw wealth and luxury, and Bruno's figure hurrying down the steps brought a satisfied smile to her lips.

Laura introduced them.

'Unfortunately, we could not find you.' Bruno's expression told Laura that he wasn't happy about unexpected guests arriving at Montiferno. Why? Had Karl given him instructions to keep Laura isolated? Was he now afraid that Anthea might take her away?

'It's quite all right,' she said, in a strangely prim voice. 'I'm sorry I wasn't here to speak to you,' she added, smiling at her stepmother, 'but it's all the more of a surprise. We'll have tea on the terrace, please,

Bruno. And I'll show Mrs Grant to her room—the guest room in the west tower, I think.'

'My, my, you've changed!' Anthea acknowledged, as Laura showed her into the room. The French windows opened on to a magnificent view nearly as good as that from her own room, except you couldn't see the town from here. But the range of mountain tops enfolded one behind the other, misty and indistinct now against the light, but in the morning every line would be crisp and clear as the sun shone on them from the east.

'I'll have some flowers put in here,' said Laura, unsure how to take Anthea's comment. 'If we'd known you were coming . . .'

'I didn't *plan* to come . . .' Anthea broke off as her suitcases arrived and a maid brought fresh towels for the bathroom. Laura mentioned the flowers . . . and then they were alone again. 'No, no, I won't *bore* you with the details,' Anthea continued, slipping off her little jacket and checking her hair in the dressing table mirror. 'When I *think* of the wretched man . . .' she shuddered.

'If you don't want to talk about it . . .' Laura began.

'They're all the same, you know.' Obviously Anthea *did* want to talk about it. And she continued to do so, while Laura showed her where everything was, while she gave her a quick tour of the house, and all the while through tea Anthea went on and on about her latest affair that had gone wrong. Apparently it was the same man she had brought to their wedding in Paris, but to be honest Laura couldn't even remember what he looked like.

So they sat for over an hour; it obviously did Anthea good to get it all off her chest, and they both watched the launch go off again, but Laura hardly gave it a second thought. Strange to be sitting here in her own home even contemplating being of help to Anthea, even more strange to be actually in a position to do so. If she wanted a little holiday, what harm would it do? They had never really got on, to put it mildly; but—well,

things were different now—there had been a shift of
emphasis somehow. For her father's sake ... But a little
voice laughed in Laura's ear and told her she was doing
this for no one but herself. With Anthea here it would
be a good excuse not to leave Karl. She could put off
the awful moment ...

'... so when *that* happened you can imagine I was
frantic,' Anthea was saying now, and Laura gave a
guilty start because she had no idea what her
stepmother had been saying. 'Everything—*gone*!'

'Everything?' Good heavens, what had Anthea been
saying? What had gone?

'Well, not the flat, of course,' Anthea continued, but
the prospect didn't seem to give her much pleasure, 'but
who the hell wants to live in Islington?' She shuddered
again. 'Oh, and there are still these department store
shares,' she added, 'but that's all. My other investments,
the last of your father's insurance money—all gone.'

'You don't mean ... ?' Laura interrupted.

'Not *embezzled*. Nothing illegal—I'm not that much
of a fool. A sound investment, he said it was.' Her red
lips twisted nastily. 'That wasn't my idea of a sound
investment.'

Laura was beginning to get the picture. Anthea had
been speculating on the stock market, helped by her
boy-friend—and had lost. 'And afterwards? I mean, did
he just walk out?'

'You think a man walks out on *me*?' Anthea rose
gracefully from her chair and strolled over to the edge
of the parapet. 'Oh no, I left him. Left him because the
poor fool can't look after himself, let alone me. And I
refuse to go back to London so soon.'

'What about? ...' Laura couldn't remember her
name, 'your friend, your old school friend that you
were travelling with?'

Anthea's lips thinned. 'She suggests I return to
London—find a job.' She turned back to face Laura.
'It's when you're in difficulties that you learn who your
friends really are.'

'I suppose so,' Laura whispered.

'And blood's thicker than water, as they say,' Anthea
continued.

Laura smiled tightly. 'Unfortunately, Karl's away at
the moment, but he'll be back tomorrow—and I'm sure
he'll be pleased to advise you.'

'I *knew* that's what you'd say!' Anthea sweeped
across and gave Laura a strange, stiff, selfconscious
little hug. 'And you'll have a word with him, won't you?
It'll sound so much better coming from you.'

'*Me?*'

'Laura darling, don't look so gauche. It doesn't
become this new image.' And for a moment she
couldn't keep the jealousy out of her eyes. 'Now, do
let's go inside and you can tell me all that you've been
up to. Well, not *all* of it,' she added with her high,
silvery laugh. 'Come on, the sun's gone in for good. Do
come and tell me all about your lovely husband.'

But it wasn't much better indoors, because Laura was
beginning to realise why Anthea had come. It wasn't for
a short, cheap holiday. It wasn't solely to recover from
a stupid business deal. Anthea wanted Karl to lend her
some money. It looked as if her usual supply of wealthy
men friends had disappeared.

They went inside and as Laura slid the glass door
closed, the sound of the launch coming alongside the
jetty broke into her thoughts. That's right—five o'clock.
That was the time the cook returned to prepare supper.
She would have to go down and see her in a minute and
let her know Anthea was allergic to shellfish.

'There's something I think you ought to know,' she
said, turning from the window and crossing the thick
pile carpet to where Anthea had settled herself on a
settee.'I know I said Karl will be happy to advise you,
but—well, I—I can't *ask* him for anything. If—if you
were thinking of a loan.'

'What do you mean, you can't ask him?' Anthea
retorted. 'Surely, as the new bride, you can still ask him
for anything.' She reached for her handbag and

rummaged for her cigarettes. 'Or is he already beginning to regret his hasty marriage?'

'It's nothing like that,' Laura lied. Or was it only partly a lie? Karl didn't like Anthea for disposing of the first Mrs Grant's paintings. And even if he and Laura had been on good terms, such a request would have fallen on deaf ears. But now, *especially* now, she couldn't go and ask Karl for money.

'Then *you'll* have to give me some,' Anthea said harshly, lighting her cigarette and blowing a cloud of smoke in Laura's direction.

'Me?'

'For heaven's sake, stop saying that! Yes, you. Why not? You're his wife, money no object—give me some of yours. It's the least you can do—your father would expect you to look after me. And I expect it after the way he tricked me into believing he was a wealthy man.'

'My father never tricked anyone. How dare you make such suggestions in *my* house!' Laura retorted. Oh lord, Anthea hadn't been here five minutes and they were arguing again.

'*Your* house? Is that a fact?' There was a faint noise out on the terrace, but Laura ignored it as Anthea's eyes blazed with anger. 'Then if it's your house there's no problem. If you can't raise the cash, sell something.' She hesitated a moment, then added with a malicious smile, 'I know you said you were marrying Karl Rievenbeck for his money, but what's the point of doing it if you can't get your hands on a little of his capital from time to time?'

'I never said ...' Laura began, her green eyes wide in anger and dismay, but she broke off as a noise behind her announced the presence of someone coming in from the terrace. She spun round, hoping they hadn't been heard. Bruno didn't usually come in that way ... Only it wasn't Bruno—it was Karl. And now he was standing in the doorway, his face a hard, tight mask; his eyes, cold and blue, penetrating her with their full strength.

'Karl——' Laura checked, 'what a lovely surprise! You weren't expected home until tomorrow.'

'So it would appear,' he said, coming across and kissing her perfunctorily on the cheek, and for a hopeless, crazy moment she wanted to fling her arms around him; she wanted to hug him and tell him she rather thought she was expecting their child. But he had already left her side and was stooping down to Anthea and giving her the same dutiful mother-in-law-type kiss.

'How—how was London?' she asked, struggling to keep up appearances, so that Anthea shouldn't guess anything was wrong.

'London?' He threw his briefcase down on a chair. He looked tired. Tall, lethally attractive, dangerously masculine—but tired. 'London was—very. successful,' he said. 'Has the Bank phoned? I've been out of touch for a couple of days.'

Out of touch? Surely he had been on Bank business? 'I—I don't know who's phoned,' said Laura, not wanting to tell him that she had been in bed for a couple of days. So if he wasn't on Bank business, where had he been? Where, or with whom? It suddenly occurred to her that she hadn't seen anything of Eleanora for several days, in fact, not since the party . . .

Tension bounced around the room and it was amazing that Anthea could look so cool and calm; why had she said such a dreadful thing? On purpose so that Karl could hear? Had Karl heard? *Of course* he had, and that was why she could feel the rage beating beneath that polished, urbane exterior. Surely he didn't *believe* Anthea? Suddenly Laura knew that somehow she had to get out of here, because it was all too painful . . .

'If you'll excuse me, I have to see Cook about the shellfish,' and she practically ran from the room and hurried down the back stairs.

But Karl was waiting for her when she came back. For a moment she paused on the back stairs and they stared at each other. 'I . . .' didn't marry you for your money, she wanted to add, but something in the coldness of his expression stopped her. 'I didn't know Anthea was coming—truly,' she said instead, but that didn't seem to be a much better alternative.

'I've brought something back for you,' he said, as if she hadn't spoken. In fact, Laura had the chilling feeling that he wouldn't bother if she didn't speak to him again.

'What do you mean?' Surely he hadn't brought her a present?

'In my study.' He turned and she hurried after him, through passageways that only he seemed to know, up more steps, down another flight, then somehow they were in the new section of the house, the section that overhung the water—or at least appeared to do so from inside. The room was dark, the blinds were down, and he pulled them up, so that she blinked for a moment at the brightness reflected up from the lake. Then there was a noise out in the hall and Bruno and one of the outside men carried a smallish crate into the room.

'You've been buying *paintings*,' said Laura, knowing that that was one of Karl's great weaknesses. 'You mean—for me? . . .'

He didn't say anything. Instead he unfastened the lid and brought out the first painting. It was fairly small, framed, covered in a blanket or something. He unwrapped it and handed it across to her. It was small enough for her to hold quite easily.

Laura stared at it for a long time and the silence in the room stretched into an eternity. Then Karl brought out another one, and another, and she put the first one down and stared at them all, three, four, five . . . six.

'I don't believe it,' she said, tears filling her eyes so that she couldn't see *anything*.

'They are the right ones?' Karl's voice seemed to come from a very long way away.

Laura nodded. There was the landscape her mother had painted in the Lake District. And another one of a seaside holiday on the south coast. And the pair of the beach tree; one in spring, one in autumn . . . all of them, all six of her mother's paintings were here.

'How——' she blinked the tears away and swallowed. 'How did you find them?' she managed to whisper at last.

He shrugged, hands in pockets, hardly looking at her, so uninterested that they might have been discussing the price of tea. 'I have—connections,' he said, his accent fractured—gravelly.

But Laura hardly heard. *Connections!* Karl Rievenbeck had the kind of connections that could trace six obscure paintings when they had been put on to the secondhand market months ago! They could have been anywhere! They could have been stashed away in some dealer's back room, or some of them sold . . . And here they all were . . . And if he had that kind of connection, if he could find things as hopelessly lost as this, then what sort of organisation would he control if it came to the finding of people? Such as runaway wives and babies?

The horror of it hit her so that she couldn't speak, couldn't move. She had known she was marrying a man with wealth and background, but a thing like this—this was taking the old pals' act dangerously far. If she was going to leave him it had better be soon, because once he knew about the baby there would be no place to hide. The world would not be big enough. Now she believed him.

At long last she realised that she ought to say something, to thank him . . . But when she came more or less to her senses and gazed stupidly round the room, he had gone.

CHAPTER TEN

LAURA found Karl in his bedroom. There was a pile of dirty shirts hurled into a corner of the room. He didn't hear her, so she stood in the doorway for a moment, gazing at him, longing for everything to be as it was. He moved with a dangerous male grace, athletically, concisely, wasting nothing, precise, controlled.

Suddenly he knew she was there, and he looked up quickly, his eyes hard and blue, registering—what?—disappointment?

'I—you didn't give me time to say thank you,' said Laura, coming awkwardly into the room, instinct telling her that this was important; if they were going to make their marriage work it would be decided now.

'How much time do you need?' he asked, his face devoid of any emotion as he went from suitcase to dressing room, and back again.

Laura stood in the middle of the room, running the belt of her dress nervously through her fingers. 'I didn't know Anthea was coming,' she tried again. 'She just turned up.'

No answer. No help. The last items came out of the case and joined the higgledy-piggledy mess on the bed.

'She's—broke.'

'Really?' He was zipping up the empty case now and leaving it for Bruno to store away.

'She wants me to lend her some money.' Lord, why was he making this so difficult?

'So?' He gave the beautiful Continental shrug that she usually loved so much. 'Why are you telling me? Give her the money—if that's what you want. I do not control how you spend your money, Laura. If it helps, consider it payment for services you have rendered to me.'

'You're twisting everything round,' she said sharply. But no, she must keep calm.

'I am twisting nothing around,' he said. 'You were telling me that Anthea Grant wants some money—I am telling you that the decision, the responsibility is yours if you have not yet spent all your allowance. Is that the position then? Do you need more? Is that why you are in my bedroom? . . .'

'I've hardly had the chance to spend any money, have I?' Laura retorted. 'I've been shut away here . . .'

'Shut away?'

'I didn't mean . . .'

'Yes, you did.' Anger licked across his face. 'What is this "shut away"? You are saying that I have kept you here against your will?'

'Of course not.' Or was she? 'But—well, it's all right for you—gallivanting . . .' He raised his eyebrows. 'Going off around the world,' she said instead, 'and I'm stuck here with no one . . .' She broke off as his eyes travelled round the luxurious room and beyond, to the view of the mountains and lake through the window.

'I see that could be quite depressing,' he said at last.

'You're being deliberately provoking! You know what I mean. Surroundings don't matter . . .'

'As long as the money keeps coming in?' he finished for her.

She had been going to say, 'it's the people that count,' but his bitter interruption froze the words on her lips. Instead she stared at him in horror. He really did believe what Anthea had said, that she had only married him for his money. How ironic! And Eleanora had *not* married him in order to keep her own money.

'You do seem to choose all the wrong women, don't you?' she said nastily, then turned quickly and hurried for the door.

But Karl was there before her, catching her arm, spinning her round, and the cool, remote anger turned to dark, violent rage. 'What did you say?' His heavy whisper somehow made the words more frightening.

'What did you say, Laura?' he repeated. 'That I have chosen the wrong woman? Is that what you believe?' His fingers bit into her arm, they hurt like hell and the prospect pleased him.

'Let me go! Think what you like.' She squirmed away, but somehow their legs twisted together, and in spite of herself, she felt the familiar excitement leap in her stomach. 'I didn't ask Anthea here, but she's more than welcome to every penny I have. I don't want your rotten money—you can't buy me!' And for a moment, the briefest of moments, Karl looked as if she had slapped him in the face.

Then his lips thinned, with a little white line around their edges. 'Then what *do* you want, Laura?' And they just stood and stared at each other with the tension bouncing between them. And there was nothing Laura could say, because if he didn't know now he never would. It had gone, everything had slipped away. He didn't know her any more. She thought of the baby and for a moment almost broke down and told him, begging him to love them both. But then, *because* of the baby, she somehow found the strength to take a deep breath, hold her head high, and stare straight into the unfathomable hardness of his blue eyes.

'I'll tell you what I want,' she said, and there wasn't a shake in her voice, not one little shake. 'I want ...' I want our baby to be born into a world of love and peace ... Only she couldn't say that—she *couldn't*.

'You don't seem to know what you do want,' said Karl, sighing, and pulling a strange, tight face, and all the while he was standing here, staring at her, *willing* her to bring her torments out into the open. Why? So that he could then dash to pieces the last of her hopes?

'I love you—and I want us to be together—like the beginning,' but the words stayed forever locked in her mind. Round and round they went, spinning in a crazy kaleidoscope of hope and despair. 'When I agreed to marry you, I didn't think it would be like this,' she said

instead. Which wasn't really what she wanted to say—
but it was some kind of truth.

'I didn't think it would be like this, either,' he said,
and his voice was quiet again; the dark rage had passed,
its place taken by a computer-like shrewdness. Laura
could almost hear his mind ticking over, assessing her
answers, considering what she would say next.

'I think I'd better get back to Anthea, she'll be
wondering . . .'

Strong blue eyes gazed down into her soul, as if he
knew the secrets she was hiding there, as if he knew she
had other answers to give him. At last she dragged her
eyes away and a tight, cynical smile strained across his
mouth.

'By all means return to your stepmother,' he said,
easily switching off their conversation. 'Please give her
my apologies for not dining with both of you tonight—
I have several days' work to catch up on.'

Laura moved towards the door, awkward, desperately
unhappy, turning away and chewing her lip so that it
shouldn't tremble. 'Thank you—for the paintings, I still
can't get over it,' she managed to mumble from the
door. But he didn't hear her because the phone started
ringing—his private line beside his bed, and as she
closed the door she heard him begin speaking in Italian,
and the one word she easily caught was—Eleanora! She
didn't see him again that night.

Early morning sun disappeared behind another cloud,
and Laura shivered.

'You're sure this is what you want to do?' asked
Tonio, moving some pebbles about with the toe of his
deck-shoe.

Laura nodded down at her twisting hands. The tissue
was well and truly shredded. 'I think it's all for the
best—eventually,' she said quietly.

Tonio picked up a stone and threw it into the water.
'You did not come for so many days,' he began, his
dark Latin good looks marred by a genuine frown.

Who did he remind her of? 'I was worried,' he
continued. 'I thought perhaps your husband had seen
us on the beach together—that he was jealous.'

Laura tried to laugh. Jealous wasn't the word;
proud and possessive more like. 'I'm the one who is
supposed to be jealous,' she said, with uncharacteristic
frankness about her personal life. Tonio looked
awkward, so she didn't continue. 'But if it's all right
with you,' she went on after a few moments, 'then I
really would like you to come early tomorrow
morning and take me away.'

'Where will you go?' At least he didn't imagine that
she wanted to go away with him.

She shrugged. 'Paris, I suppose. To begin with.
After that . . .' Then she realised that she shouldn't
have said so much. Carl and his connections . . . 'But
I might not,' she added hastily. 'I don't really
know . . .'

'You think I will tell someone?' Tonio asked, and
instead of sounding cross he seemed almost fatalistic.

Laura frowned, aware, yet unsure, of the under-
currents swirling beneath the surface of this man—
boy—whom she hardly knew. Tonio de Vito. Where
did he come from? What was he really doing here?
Why had he spent so much time with her this summer,
when it was perfectly obvious she wasn't interested in
him as a person? Or was she being unfair? Did he have
to have some ulterior motive? Perhaps she was being
over-sensitive. With all her problems she couldn't
really think straight.

They went for a stroll. She had told him Karl was at
home, but was working, and the chances of him coming
out here were practically nil. So they walked to the
other end of the island, near the ruined castle, and for a
while the sun came out and it was really warm again, so
they sat in the shade of the ancient ruins, silent and
remote, the castle and themselves, each locked in their
own miseries, each locked in separate centuries of
distrust.

And that was what it was really all about—distrust. Karl loved Eleanora and had married Laura for all the wrong reasons. Funny, but she had only just realised the similarity of their names. And a marriage had to be built on trust, hadn't it? Because there were so many opportunities for disloyalty that if there wasn't trust it would drive the other partner mad.

Yet something else had driven Laura mad last night. Alone in her large double bed, she had tossed and turned and wanted Karl . . . The agony of the memory returned to taunt her, so that she couldn't see the mountains and the castle behind her, mirrored in the blue lake. Instead she felt the loneliness again, felt the craving for him, felt the empty, hollow despair of knowing her husband was sleeping in his own room, as he had really planned on doing from the very beginning of their marriage. Honestly, who heard of a man and wife having separate bedrooms these days? Even if the family did have aristocratic connections. It was ridiculous, mediaeval. She thought of those five Rievenbeck brothers and all the women in their lives. And she wanted Karl. She wanted him to herself with a blind fury that was frightening. She wanted him to love her, to sleep with her, to make love to her—night after night—and she wanted their child to be brought up in a *home*, not a house. And if she couldn't have all that, then she couldn't stay here and torment herself with his closeness. She couldn't bear to hear the strong resonance of his voice speak to other women, to say their names in that particular way he had. She couldn't subject herself to such torture—and still expect her baby to be healthy and happy, when its mother was slowly dying from a broken heart.

Which meant the only alternative was to leave with Tonio in the morning. He would take her ashore before anyone else was up. And if that was leaving everyone in turmoil; Karl—Anthea—then that was a pity, but their hard luck. She had herself to think about now—herself as mother of Karl's child . . . And in this dreadful moment of heart-searching agony that was the only dawning of light she could hold on to.

'I'm very pleased you came to the island,' she said to Tonio, as they made their way back to the beach. 'What would I have done without you?' But he only smiled weakly, and she frowned. 'What's the matter?'

He shrugged, his dark Roman eyes unsure, disturbed.

'Do you think Carl will find out about you? Make things awkward? . . .' His expression remained enigmatic, almost as if he *knew* he was going to be discovered.

Laura sighed. 'Look, if you don't want to, all right—but say so.'

'No—no.' He gesticulated expressively. Didn't they always say that if you tied an Italian's hands behind his back he would be unable to speak? Eleanora had the same habit, those beautiful hands with their long nails . . . Laura forcibly stopped herself thinking about Eleanora.

'I do not go back on my word,' Tonio said firmly. 'But Karl Rievenbeck is a proud man.'

'You *are* scared . . . No, I didn't mean that. Look, Tonio——' she put a placating hand on his arm, 'I do understand, believe me . . .' But in the end he stayed firm to his promise, and the arrangement was made for him to meet her back here at seven o'clock the following morning.

Only there was still the rest of today to get through, a day filled with Anthea—and by some evil design, a day filled with Karl as well.

Why couldn't he have gone away today—to Milan, or somewhere? But no. Today he seemed to be making up for lost time—or was he staying around just to keep up appearances because Anthea was there?

'Is anything the matter?' her stepmother asked after lunch, when Karl had kissed Laura formally on the cheek again, and had said that he had to get back to his study.

'What do you mean?' Laura snapped.

'Nothing at all, darling,' she almost crooned, settling

back in the deep armchair and sipping her coffee. 'This really does beat Islington any day. Have you spoken to Karl yet about—what we were talking about?'

The complete change in the conversation caught Laura off guard. 'Yes—I mean . . .'

'And what did he say?' Anthea's sharp eyes hooked into her over the top of her coffee cup.

'He—I—didn't decide anything,' Laura blurted.

Anthea didn't seem put out. 'I can wait,' she said smugly. 'Let's just call this a little family visit, shall we?'

So all the afternoon Laura had the strain of Anthea's company, trying to answer questions and appear intelligent, when all the time her brain was in a whirl of hare-brained cottonwool. This was her last day, her last night . . . Tomorrow she would be heaven knows where . . .

The idea crept up on her slowly. At first it was the merest flash of remembrance, as Karl joined them for tea and her eyes rested on the tall, imposing figure, imposing even while wearing cream slacks and a casual shirt. She handed him a cup of tea and as he leant nearer she caught the tang of his aftershave; that was when the idea first came.

And it grew. As he sat quietly watching him talking with Anthea, as she replied briefly to his questions as he tried to draw her into the conversation. The idea blossomed. Dared she? And later, through supper, in the elegance of the dining room, all carved wood panelling, glistening silver and sparkling chandeliers . . . the idea developed into a burning desire, a need deep inside her that had to be satisfied for the last time.

She gazed down the long table that separated them as completely as he had separated from her in his soul. But she would never be free—never. There would be no other man—not like this. And tonight . . . she sighed quietly to herself, her heart already breaking, tonight he looked so particularly—*Karl*. Karl Rievenbeck. Banker, aristocrat, who had so much urbane sophistication—who was so sure of himself, who knew exactly how to dress, who would sit down for a family supper like this, surrounded by the wealthy extravagance of generations, but there was such a charm about him, a comfort-ableness towards his guests; a sort of inbred desire to put everyone at their ease. In spite of his wealth and position—wasn't that the trait which had attracted her most? And sitting there she remembered the simple lunch at the Louvre, the picnic on the Seine—and how he hadn't told her who he was, how he had seemed to want only what would make her happy.

Had it really all been nothing but pretence? She sipped some wine, her throat suddenly dry.

'Are you feeling well?' Karl asked. She could have sworn he was in deep conversation with Anthea.

'I've had a cold while you were away, that's all,' she said, realising, too late, that in any normal relationship her husband would have discovered she had a cold last night.

Anthea didn't miss it. Her sharp eyes flew from one to the other of them, and she hid a smile beneath her napkin. 'I do hope you two haven't quarrelled on my account,' she said, obviously relishing the fact that they had.

Which only made things worse, because for the rest of the evening Karl didn't take his eyes off Laura, and she was wondering what devil had made her choose the dress she knew he especially liked. It was a little flimsy chiffon affair, with thin strappy shoulders, all loose and floating in swirly colours of green.

Bruno had served coffee in the drawing room; the evenings were beginning to draw in, and he closed the curtains, soft table lamps made the large, impressive proportions of the room seem almost cosy.

'Brandy?' asked Karl, pouring one for himself and Anthea. Laura shook her head, and he frowned. 'It will be good for the cold.'

But would it be good for the baby? Her lip trembled and she bit it. Had she really packed two nylon holdalls? Were they really upstairs hiding in her cupboard? Was she really going to run away tomorrow?

She went to put her cup back on the trolley and Karl did the same—getting there as she did. They bumped into each other and Laura automatically whispered, 'Sorry.'

Karl took her arm gently, his fingers warm and firm, making her bare arm tingle. 'Are you all right?'

'Of course.'

'Shall I send Anthea away?' he asked in an undertone. 'I'm only being polite for your sake.'

'No!' she hissed back in a whisper. Honestly, this was crazy! There they were like husband and wife, whispering secrets in a corner, when really he didn't love her, really all he wanted was Eleanora, someone who could fit into this grand life—who knew how to organise his parties.

'I'm just a little tired . . .'

'Then why don't you go to bed?' His voice was deep, husky, with an undercurrent that she now knew so well. She could feel his eyes on her, willing her to look up at him, and there would be a question in his eyes, a question that said. 'I'll come to your room——' And wasn't that exactly what she had been thinking about all evening? 'I—I think I will,' she said, still not looking at him; her hands busy straightening the cups and cream jug. 'You don't mind, do you, Anthea,' she called out in a louder, rather tight, squeaky voice, 'if I have an early night . . .?' And somehow she got out of the room without breaking down. That was it. The last day— over. Now all she had to do was get through the night.

Should she do it? Dared she? Suppose he didn't want her? How would she live the rest of her life with the humiliation? Perhaps his concern had been because of Anthea . . . She lay awake with the light off, listening for footsteps, wondering how Anthea was getting on with him. Funny, but she wasn't the least jealous of her stepmother. Was it because she knew Karl didn't like her? Or was it because she knew he had someone else?

At last she heard his footsteps coming along the carpeted landing. He went into the dressing room first, as he always did, and she could imagine him stripping off his clothes, flinging things into the washing basket, standing tall and naked, the strong masculine shape of him a torment to her frustrated mind.

She screwed up her eyes, but the image wouldn't disappear. She wanted to reach out and touch him, she wanted to have him here beside her, to feel the long hard length of his virile body pressed closely against hers.

A little cry escaped her lips and for a moment she wondered if he might hear. Her heart began pounding and the blood throbbed through her veins. She willed him to open the door, to come to her—and half of her dreaded him doing so—because how could she find the strength to leave in the morning once he had possessed her again?

He didn't come. After a while the light went out under the dressing room door—but that didn't mean she couldn't go to him! Laura struggled out of bed, fighting with the covers that perversely wanted to trap her. She switched on the light, going over to the long mirror. Would he want her? She stared at her reflection critically, remembering Paris again and the first time they had made love. Then, Karl had undressed her ... Laura warmed at the memory, little sparks of excitement licking deep inside. If that hadn't been love on his part it had been a very good imitation. Surely a man didn't have to go to such lengths? And would the memory of that work for him too? If she just opened the door and climbed into his bed ... would he be able to resist her? For a while couldn't she pretend that his expertise was love?

She raked her fingers through her tumbled blonde curls and moistened her lips, remembering those dark, wonderful secrets he had taught her. Then her face crumbled, knowing she couldn't go through tonight alone—she *couldn't*. She had to have this last chance with him—the consequences would have to be suffered later.

But she didn't have the courage to go in to him naked, so she slipped on her broderie anglaise negligee, fastening the little bows with fingers that were trembling. Then, heart in mouth, she tiptoed across the dressing room, her hand closing around his bedroom door handle. Slowly, quietly, she twisted it ... The door opened, the room was in utter blackness and for a moment she thought no one was there. But then there was a movement, and a muffled sort of sound from the bed, and suddenly the little light was switched on, and Karl was resting upon one elbow, staring at her.

She couldn't speak. Neither, it appeared, could he. But at least he wasn't forcibly hurling her from the room. Taking courage, she swallowed, closed the door carefully behind her, and tiptoed across the thick, silencing carpet ... His little bedside clock measured her steps as harsh blue eyes followed her around the bed ... She hesitated for only a moment, her fingers on the bedcover, her eyes holding his, willing him to let her stay. Praying he wouldn't reject her.

He didn't. But he didn't help her either. At last she slipped in beside him, and she was really shaking now, not just her hands. The soft light fell on his broad, naked shoulder and powerful chest. Oh, how the sight of him excited her! She could almost taste him, her senses were filled with the intoxicating, musky virility that made her body cry out for his possession. And still he didn't move—didn't reach for her.

Her fingers shook as she sat beside him, half kneeling really, her full bottom lip soft and vulnerable as she began undoing the little bows down the front of her negligee ...

He watched the first bow come undone ... then the second, revealing the smooth, creamy valley between her breasts, and still he didn't move ... Laura was in a state now, the tension rife between them. Karl's face was harsh, his blue eyes cold and wary ... The third bow stuck in a knot, and Laura bit her lip in frustration, her fingers shaking too much to manipulate

the thin strands ... Eventually she gave a little cry of
annoyance and glanced up at him, and she couldn't
read the expression on his face; he seemed angry,
amazed, contemptuous—but he wanted her. She sensed
his battle of conflicting emotions struggling beneath the
surface.

At last he moved; he reached forward with both
hands and there was a sharp tearing sound as he ripped
the tie off the negligee. But that was all. He didn't say
anything, didn't make any move for her—just lay back
again, leaning on his elbow, but the light in his eyes had
changed. The shrewd hardness now held the merest hint
of a challenge. And she met that challenge, slowly
slipping the broderie anglaise wrap off her shoulders.

How often had she done this before? Countless times.
And Karl had buried his face in her breasts and had
drawn her down on top of him ... Why didn't he do
that now? What else could she do? And so slowly, very
slowly, Laura leaned forward and kissed him. It was
only a very little kiss, just a brief touch of her lips
against the strong, moulded shape of his own. Then she
kissed him again, more slowly, languorously, her teeth
tugging at his lower lip, her breasts brushing against his
chest ...

He reacted, reluctantly, aggressively, his hand coming
up her back. The kiss went on and on, deeper, stronger,
and he was kissing her now—unable to resist the deep
tide of sexuality rising in them both.

Everything was going to be all right. Almost weeping
with joy, Laura moaned as Karl slid her down under the
covers, his body warm and hard, wanting her, easing
over her, his hands sensitively rousing her just like the
first time ... Only it wasn't like the first time—or all
those other times, because now there was a poignant
sweetness; it was to be the last time. And there was
another difference. He didn't speak. Normally he
whispered delicious secrets ... Yet this time—nothing.
But she couldn't complain because he was ... oh, how
she *loved* that ...

'I knew you wouldn't be able to stay away...' At last he broke the silence, his voice deep and strong, touched with an edge of triumph. 'You know how it is between us—how it will always be...' and she moaned as his hand slid down the long, curvacious shape of her hip and thigh.

Oh yes, she knew—knew that if she didn't leave after tonight, there would be no peace—no tranquillity. Life would be a torment of nights like this—nights when their need for each other's bodies couldn't be denied... and days of torment wondering who he was with now...

'Tell me how much you want me,' Karl was whispering now. 'Tell me...' But she couldn't answer because he was kissing her again, his lips harder, the tension and passion rising up in a vortex of male aggression.

He wasn't going to wait. By now she knew the signs of his virile appetite. They hadn't made love since the party, a week ago. And that was a long time for Karl... a long time for herself. His lips were moving urgently down to her breasts, but they didn't linger there, didn't drive her wild with delight. There wasn't time... His knee was nudging the inside of her thigh. She tried to resist; a bit longer, *please*——

'No,' she whispered, 'not yet.' But he didn't believe her, or didn't want to believe her. Or maybe he just didn't care. Because she could feel the pounding of his heart against her breasts, could feel his aroused passion burning for possession. A hand slid beneath her body as he drew her remorselessly towards him. 'No,' she tried again, and yet, in spite of it, her body was ready for him, clamouring for him...

'Don't stay away again,' he almost growled, then he took her, urgently, savagely, with no thought of gentleness, so that she cried out and clung to him, shuddering with delight as the powerful body moved in a deep, remorseless rhythm.

And for once there was nothing else she could do,

except cling on to him and ride the storm ... because this time he wasn't thinking of her, he didn't read her body or wait for the signs, this time he drove himself to the height, and instead of clinging on to her and calling her name with joy, when the end came he burrowed his head into the pillow, muffling his groan, lost in a world of his own making.

And all Laura could do was to lie there and hold him, with tears in her eyes, chewing her lip, breathless and sore, wanting, oh, so badly, for him to love her ... to have thought of her ... And yet there had been pleasure in him being there, in the magnificent possession of his body, in the smell and taste and feel of him strong and heavy in her arms. And she really didn't mind that this time it hadn't worked—love couldn't be counted, couldn't be qualified. Loving was giving—She bit back a sob. Only this was the last time—and *why* hadn't he made it perfect? ...

He seemed to be asleep, so she reached down and pulled the covers up over his damp back. He was heavy on her. Heavy, but oh, so wonderful, so incredible. She lay there savouring every precious moment, the sound of him breathing, deep and strong, the powerful, taut muscles relaxed now, peaceful. Laura smoothed his ruffled hair, let her fingers brush lightly across his shoulders. But it wasn't real. It was all a pretence, she was simply kidding herself. Pretending they had been warm and close, when really Karl had stayed in his own private world, his desire for her no more than that of a virile man for an attractive woman. What red-blooded man could have turned away such a tempting offer? It didn't really mean anything to him. Yet for her? Ah, for her it was all she would have to remember ...

Only one of her legs was going to sleep, and as she tried to wriggle it over, Karl stirred and woke up. 'Did I hurt you?' he mumbled, giving her head a little shake, and drowsily propping himself up on his elbows.

His face was soft, full, ruffled. Laura gazed up at him and shook her head.

'Sure?'

'Yes.'

A little ironical smile twisted his lips. 'Can't remember when that happened last.'

'When what happened?' she asked.

He smiled again, looking quizzically sheepish, his sudden vulnerability making her love him all the more. 'Usually I can control myself . . .' he went on quietly.

She grinned. 'It doesn't matter.'

'Doesn't it?' Then his eyes were serious again, looking down at her, easing himself away so that he could see more of her. 'But you did not . . .?'

'There's more to making love than a mind-blowing orgasm,' she said, with the simple directness he had taught her during their lovemaking.

'Maybe you are right . . .' His body moved irresistibly against her. 'But I think perhaps this time . . .' And it began again; warm and mellow this time, smooth, gentle . . . On and on, tirelessly, remorselessly.

Laura moved luxuriously, voluptuously, beneath him. Loving every minute of it, not wanting him to stop . . .

He made love to her all night. And whenever she tried to take the initiative he would rob her of it, rolling her off him, his weight pushing her back into the pillows. On and on, excitement threequarters the way to oblivion, but always he held her back from the ultimate surrender. Held her back so that she could travel with him down a never-ending tunnel of sensuous, sexual delight. But it was more than that for her—much more. Because in their quiet moments when the dawn on the mountain peaks had not yet reached the valleys, Laura knew that she had come to an irrevocable decision. A decision, the price of which could only be measured during a lifetime of heartbreak and love.

CHAPTER ELEVEN

AT last Karl slept, and Laura lay beside him in the great bed, her body replete and exhausted, yet the turmoil in her mind making it impossible to rest. She was crazy, of course; condemning herself to a life where she would always be second best.

She turned her head and gazed lovingly at the ruffled dark head on the pillow beside her. Okay, so he had married her for all the wrong reasons—and he still wanted Eleanora, but that was something she was going to have to live with. Because now, after the magic of his lovemaking, Laura knew she would never find the strength to leave. She closed her eyes, remembering it all, the way his body had seemed to worship her, the way his magnificent male virility had captured and held her in a wonderful world of their own making. And if he hadn't loved her, then he had *seemed* to do so, and she would have to learn to make that enough. In Paris, when she had contemplated the dizzying differences of their positions, she had decided that their love had to be given a chance. Well, if that love wasn't quite what she expected, that was her hard luck. Now she knew she would rather be second best in Karl's life, if second best was to be like last night. . . . What woman wouldn't settle for such a man—on any terms? And during the bad patches, when she would have to think of Eleanora—well, that would be the time to find consolation in this child. Her hand slid up to her stomach. And perhaps there would be another . . . Only she would have to be careful not to smother them with love as a compensation . . . And there was still her painting; she would continue her studies—she would insist on that.

A grey early morning light was filtering through the

curtains, and suddenly Laura realised how late it was. Heavens, Tonio might already be here! Somehow she had to get down to the beach and tell him she wasn't going.

It wasn't easy. Slipping out of bed and quickly dressing in jeans and tee-shirt was bad enough, but imagine being trapped inside by the servants! She dared not go out of the back door because that was in a passageway near the kitchen, and they were bound to see her. The front door was too dangerous because she would never unfasten all the locks and bolts without being discovered, and one of the maids was already tidying the drawing room, so she couldn't slip out on to the terrace that way.

So she hung about in Karl's study, desperately aware that precious minutes were ticking by, and with each one came the possibility of Karl discovering what she was doing. She sat on the edge of the desk, then paced backwards and forwards, surprised that her mother's paintings were still here, then remembering that they had decided to keep them out of the way while Anthea was still here ... What should she do about Anthea? Should she give her some money?

There was a noise out in the hall, and Laura hurried to the door. Good. The maid had gone, the drawing room was clear. And it only took a few moments to race over to the big sliding doors which had been unlocked now, thank goodness. Along the terrace and down the steps, her heart hammering in case Karl should wake and look out of the window. It was getting on for eight o'clock. She was late. How clear it was this morning; the dark, sharp clarity that went with heavy clouds and the prospect of rain. As she ran she heard the launch chug-chugging towards the jetty. But a glance told her it wasn't their launch, this one was older, scruffier, the sort that could be hired at the public pier. Laura didn't take that much notice of it; it was probably the vegetables arriving. Then she dived into the shrubbery and ran along the dark, overgrown path, the launch and its possible occupants forgotten.

When she reached the beach there was no sign of Tonio. Was he late? Had he been and gone? Had he changed his mind and decided not to come after all?

Sighing, unsure whether to hang around or not, she sat down on a rock, elbows on knees, chin in her hands, staring out across the calm, grey stillness of the early morning lake. How different it looked today, heavy, grey—yet with an even more majestical beauty. Surely this had to be the most beautiful place on earth . . . And then she saw it—Tonio's boat—bobbing round the headland, coming from a different direction this time.

She jumped up, waving her arms, yet glancing guiltily over her shoulder, as if expecting someone to be there.

'I thought you'd changed your mind,' she called out, as Tonio brought the dinghy right up on to the beach. She helped him drag it clear of the water, and it heeled over like a stranded whale, its blue and white sail flapping in extra distress.

He looked on edge, nervous—somehow angry, his dark Latin eyes on the rocks and trees that bordered the little beach. 'Where are your things?' he asked, suddenly realising he couldn't see any baggage.

Laura didn't know whether to be apologetic or cheerful. 'Look,' she began, aware that it was getting on for the time Karl normally got up, when he wasn't working, 'I don't know how to say this—and you've been very kind . . .'

'You are not coming—you have changed your mind?' and when she obviously had, Tonio began laughing, a high, bright, hysterical laugh that somehow ended in anger, and he stared at Laura as if he suddenly hated her.

'Tonio, what's the matter? I thought you'd be pleased.'

'*Pleased!* You think after all this—when I was so close——' but he broke off, staring behind her . . . and there was the sound of footsteps on the gravel, footsteps running . . .

Laura swung round, dreading who it might be, yet

knowing it could only be Karl. But it wasn't only Karl.
There were two people; Karl first, but behind him a
woman, a dark-haired woman—not Anthea. Through
her sudden panic, Laura realised it was Eleanora. What
on earth was she doing here? How had she known?

'Thank God we are not too late!' The Contessa spoke
in her clear, impeccable English, as she scrambled after
Karl. But it was on her husband that Laura's eyes were
riveted. Her husband, whom she had left in bed not half
an hour ago. Her husband, who had loved her all
night . . . But there was no love in his face now, no
concern, no understanding. She saw anger; blind
devouring anger, that almost deformed his face into
wild savagery.

'If you have touched my wife I will kill you!' and it
took both Laura and Eleanora to restrain him as he
made a wild dive for Tonio.

'Stop it, Karl! For God's sake,' Laura screamed, but
he wasn't listening.

'What are you doing here?' And then he broke into a
string of aggressive Italian, forcing the younger man back.

'It is all my fault,' Eleanora pleaded. 'I knew he had
someone. He told me all about it.' She was still clinging
to Karl, her dark hair swinging loose for a change,
although in tight cream pants and expensive cotton-knit
sweater she looked as elegant as ever. 'But I did not
dream it was Laura. If I had known who . . .' She broke
off in obvious distress.

What on earth was Eleanora talking about? Did she
know Tonio? What had he told her? Why? Sudden rage
rose in Laura's throat; rage because she was beginning
to understand what might have happened.

Tonio was speaking now, in Italian, fast and
excitable, his hands waving distractedly. Pointing over
to the dinghy, pointing at Laura. On and on . . . a
barrage of words she couldn't understand, and Karl's
face was white, and he was drawing himself upright,
holding his breath—and he only did that when he was
excruciatingly mad.

Now it was the Contessa's turn, and she was practically screaming at Tonio, in Italian as well; was it all some plot to drive Laura completely out of her mind?

'Would someone mind telling me what's going on?' she shouted, to make herself heard above the noise, and there was immediate, complete silence as everyone spun round and stared at her.

'We will discuss this inside.' Karl's accent was thick. 'Wait for me in my study, Laura.'

'I shall do no such thing. Have you all gone mad? Tonio isn't trespassing, because I *said* he could come here,' and she glared at Karl, daring him to defy her authority as his wife. 'And perhaps someone would like to tell me—in *English*—what Eleanora is doing here!'

Karl opened his mouth to speak, but the Contessa beat him to it.

'It is all my fault,' she began again, imploring Laura to understand—forgive her. 'I did not realise that you felt so much alone. A friend I have tried to be—a confidante—but still I did not see, did not realise, that you had taken a lover.'

'*Lover!*' Laura repeated. Karl made a strangled sort of sound and Tonio backed off again. 'You're mad!' she retorted, her green eyes wide with disbelief, glaring at this woman who was still holding on to Karl in some misguided belief that she was stopping him from becoming violent. 'It isn't like that at all. Tell them, Tonio!' but even the fact that she knew the young Italian's name seemed to enrage Karl all the more.

'How long? How may times?' The words were rung out of him, then he immediately regretted it, and Laura realised how distasteful such a scene must be to him.

Well, it was distasteful to her as well. But worse was the guilt—because there was a certain amount of truth . . . 'I still want to know what this has got to do with Eleanora!' she demanded angrily. 'What's she doing here?'

'I'm trying to stop you making a terrible mistake.'

The Contessa's dark eyes were full of concern. 'My brother has done this kind of thing before. I should never have invited him. He comes to the lake only to see a boat, or so he tells me.'

'Your brother?' Laura interrupted, staring from Eleanora to Tonio, seeing in each the resemblance of dark, Latin good looks that she had stupidly imagined belonged to all Romans. Now it was obvious; they had the same eyes, the same sensuous mouth. Tonio was an inch or two taller—and he wasn't looking at Laura; in fact, he looked pretty sick.

'What have you told her? Did she promise to buy you the boat if you . . .' Tonio still couldn't meet Laura's eyes, but it was all too much for Karl, who broke away from the Contessa and practically lifted Laura off the ground.

'You will go back to the house *now*!' he snarled. His fingers were shaking with anger, in fact his whole body was on fire with a deep suppressed rage. 'I will talk to you later—but first I want to deal with . . .'

'No—you must not!' Now Eleanora broke in, tugging at Karl's arm again, while screaming more abuse at Tonio in Italian. 'You must not blame Laura,' she said to Karl in English. 'I should have seen . . .' But all the while there was a gleam of satisfaction behind her superficial concern, and Laura realised that somehow Eleanora had planned all this; that Tonio had agreed to try and seduce Laura, or *appear* to have seduced her— and if he succeded his very wealthy sister would buy him that powerboat.

But before she could voice her suspicions, Karl was pushing Eleanora away, grabbing Laura again and practically hauling her back towards the house.

How dared he! Laura struggled and tried to break free, not caring that Eleanora and Tonio were following, supposedly in the middle of a heated argument, but Laura didn't believe a word of it now. It was all put on. And Karl believed everything Eleanora, his *mistress*, told him. He obviously wasn't even interested in what Laura had to say, as he practically dragged her through the shrubbery and up the terrace steps.

And then, to make matters worse, Anthea came panicking out of the drawing room, her dressing gown flapping, her long red hair tied into a scarf. 'Oh, thank God you're safe!' she cried, swooping on Laura, hugging her, kissing her cheek. 'I heard a woman arriving,' she ranted on, 'and there was shouting and someone said you'd gone out in a boat. And I know how you *hate* boats—and I thought you'd been drowned!' She was almost hysterical, gazing at Laura as if she had been brought back from the dead. 'You're not wet—did someone rescue you?' She smiled vaguely at Tonio, her obvious choice as rescuer, and she was oblivious to everything else; to Laura's astonishment, to Eleanora's annoyance, and to Karl's steaming temper as he ran distracted hands through his ruffled hair.

'Laura is perfectly safe, as you can see,' he said, controlling his voice with difficulty. 'Now, if you wouldn't mind leaving us,' he said, as everyone went inside, but it was perfectly clear that Anthea had no intention of leaving anyone. At last her eyes flashed around the incongruous little group.

'Just what the hell's going on?' she demanded, her hands going round Laura's shoulders. 'You're shivering.' Vicious eyes snapped at Karl. 'What have you been doing to her?'

'Nothing, really, Anthea.' Laura broke away, trying to be reassuring. 'It's just a bit of a family squabble.'

'*I'm* family,' Anthea reminded her, 'and I'll not have you treated ...' Concern for Laura or concern for Laura's money made little difference once Anthea Grant dug into a fight.

'Please, Anthea, there's no need,' Laura interrupted, because Karl looked as if he was going to explode, and—oh lord, here was Bruno to see how many people were staying for breakfast!

Karl dealt with him and there was silence until the

middle-aged manservant had gone. Then the room vibrated with erupting conversation.

'What's been going on—were you running away?' asked Anthea.

'It's all a mistake,' Laura tried. 'Tell them, Tonio!'

'If everyone would stay *calm*,' Eleanora added on top of all this.

'What do you want me to tell them?' Tonio asked Laura.

'The *truth*!' she shouted, and her raised voice silenced the rest of the room, where everyone was still rattling on in their own language. All except Karl, that was, who looked as if he didn't trust himself to speak.

'But I have already told the truth,' said Tonio, glancing at his sister, and Laura was quick to catch her flash of approval. 'You asked me to come and fetch you this morning—you wanted to leave your husband . . .'

Laura felt sick and the room spun.

'If my stepdaughter was running away, it was because you treated her badly,' Anthea broke in, glaring at Karl, then running over to Laura and putting her arms around her again. 'I knew something was the matter when I arrived,' she almost cheered, settling Laura in a chair, then marching over to Karl and practically poking him in the chest. 'I'm not a fool,' she said, 'I can see how things are,' and she glared at Eleanora, suddenly recognising her intimate position. 'Divorce him,' she said, turning back to Laura, her face ugly, vehement. 'Sue him for every penny!'

'That's enough!' Karl roared, and suddenly he wasn't over by the windows, silhouetted dark and strong against the grey morning light, but he was striding across the room, lifting Laura forcibly out of the chair, his fingers biting cruelly into her arms. 'Take them away,' he said, addressing himself to Eleanora. 'Both of them.' His face was savage, dangerous, muscles jerking in both cheeks. 'Get them off this island before . . . or I won't be responsible!'

'But——' Eleanora began, and this was obviously not the way she had intended events to happen.

'Please!' The one word bit the air. And when she still looked unconvinced, Karl let go of Laura and strode over to his mistress, putting both hands firmly on her shoulders. 'Please,' he repeated, in a strong, fathomless voice, 'for me.' And finally Eleanora agreed, smiled and kissed his cheek. Anthea exploded and Laura had to look away.

'You can't turn me off this island! I demand to stay with my daughter,' Anthea began.

'Your *step*daughter is now my wife and she will do as I say—visitors only come to this island at my request. You have not been invited . . .'

'Karl . . .'

'Do not interrupt me, Laura. And *you*,' he went on, turning to Tonio, controlling himself with difficulty, so that Eleanora had to hang on to him again. 'You will leave this house now—and you will never come back. *Never*—unless you wish . . .'

'Carlo, *Caro*,' and then the Contessa lapsed into a string of dark, sensuous Italian, obviously trying to calm him, with the wealth of ten years' experience behind her. *Ten years!* Laura picked up a cushion from one of the sofas and hurled it at them.

Then she was gone, racing out of the sliding door and along the terrace, because she couldn't bear all this, couldn't stand hearing everyone tearing her life to pieces. Her life! Didn't last night mean anything to Karl? Could he so easily take Eleanora's word against her own? And Tonio's betrayal—oh, that was too much! She had to get away . . . Along the terrace and down the steps. But she didn't reach the bottom, someone was chasing her—catching her.

'Let me go. Go back to *her*!' But Karl had his arm around her and was carrying her back up.

'We have to talk.'

'I've got nothing to say to you! It's all been said. If you take me back inside, I'll *scream*!'

'Then scream. Who do you think will hear you?' And somehow he manoeuvred her back into the drawing room, which was empty now, across the hall and over to his study ... kicking the door shut behind him. Laura escaped over to the window.

'Now we will have the truth.' His voice bit into the silence of the room, and she turned back in time to see him still passing a hand across his face. He looked dreadful, shattered, his eyes dull and heavy, his normally immaculate image, rough, earthy—neolithic.

'What can I say that you don't already know?' she said angrily. 'You've made up your mind. You'd rather believe Eleanora, so,' she shrugged, 'go ahead.'

'I do not *believe* anyone. I see only the facts before me.' He paced over to the desk, moving papers—seeing nothing.

'Facts!' Laura shouted, because she couldn't stand his contained, ruthless strength. Was this how he dealt with his business clients? No compassion, no humanity? 'The facts are that you saw me on the beach, talking to Tonio ...'

'Never mention that name!' He swung round, anger darkening his face. 'And you wish to tell me it was a—a coincidence?'

Laura swallowed, and wiped her palms down the legs of her jeans. 'Not—exactly ...'

'So you had arranged to meet—that man?'

She looked away. 'Sort of.'

'What is that supposed to mean?'

'Not what you think,' she said quietly.

'Then tell me what to think,' he said, in a strange sort of voice she didn't recognise.

'I—wanted to give him a message,' she struggled on.

'How many times have you met him before?'

Laura shrugged again; the Continental habit was catching. 'I don't know—several. I didn't plan anything. He was just *there* one day.' There one day! Lord, what a fool she had been never to suspect. Of course he had inside information; always turning up when Karl was away—and not caring if Eleanora had seen him as she left the island the day after the party.

'And did you not think to tell him that this was a private island?'

'He probably thought that as he was your mistress's brother that gave him some sort of *entrée*,' she snapped, and he didn't like that—it was too near the truth.

'You still haven't told me what the message was,' came his ruthless reply.

She turned away, pacing up and down. There was a lot of chattering and banging going on upstairs—and some of the servants seemed to be arguing. 'I . . .' she began.

'The truth,' and it came out in a thick, heavy, broken accent.

'I—told him I'd changed my mind,' Laura managed to say at last, and instead of crying and staring down at her belt, she raised her head proud and defiant, daring to meet the brittle coldness of his eyes.

'So you *had* planned to go away with him.' It was an accusation, not a question.

'No—yes, but not . . .' Maybe if she told Karl she was jealous of Eleanora, maybe he would understand.

'I've heard enough,' and he turned away, his back rigid with rage. Then it was too much for him and he spun round, marching back to her, as she leaned against the desk for support. She was perfectly sure he was going to hit her . . . but his fist came crashing down on the desk instead. 'Why?' he roared. 'I mean—why change your mind?' Their eyes locked, held, and they were mesmerised in a misery of remembering every intimate detail of last night.

Laura stared and stared at him, willing him to understand, praying that her love must have shown, that she couldn't have pretended, that surely he must know how much she loved him . . .

But now he was backing off—laughing—staring up at

the ceiling and running aggressive fingers through his tumbled hair.

'But of course—now I understand,' and although he was laughing at himself, there was a bitterness, a contempt in his eyes when he stared down at her again. 'Your timing misfired, is that not so?' he began, with dark menace in his voice. 'You married me for my money—but had Anthea decided that she hadn't yet had her share?' Laura stared open-mouthed, white-faced, as his eyes travelled slowly over her shapely figure. 'Do not think I am complaining,' he continued, insults dripping from every word. 'I am willing to pay a great deal for having a woman like you in my bed. You have a great charm, Laura. A *supposed* innocence mingled with an instinctive knowledge of what pleases a man. And what passion!' he added, catching hold of her chin and forcing her face up to meet his. 'But such, I believe, are normally the talents acquired by women who marry for money. Tell me, my dear, who taught you? I ought to thank him.'

Shock, rage, near total collapse threatened Laura as he walked away from her, and she knew she had to say something to get rid of him fast, before she broke down completely.

'I'm glad you realise that there's no difference between marrying for money—and *not* marrying for money!' she shouted, throwing the Contessa right up into his face. And almost beside herself with fury, she picked up a heavy glass paperweight from the desk and hurled it at him.

She never knew how it missed him; as it hit the door it dented the wood, chipped the paint, and fell with a heavy thud on to the thick pile carpet. Karl's face went white and muscles in his taut cheeks broke into a spasm as the thickening silence threatened to overcome them both.

'When you can conduct yourself with the dignity that befits my wife, then—and only then—will I discuss this matter again. Until such time, I suggest you keep your own company.' He moved over to the door, picked up the paperweight, but hesitated from leaving the room. 'I am going to ensure that de Vito and your stepmother leave this island immediately. Eleanora might need some help. You can contact Anthea in your own time. You will have all the money you need—you can do with it as you wish. But you will not see that man again. And I suggest you keep out of the way until everyone has gone.' He paused, stared down at the paperweight and then brought it over to her. 'Here, take this—throw it again if it helps,' and then he was gone, and her fingers closed around the smooth glass sphere and she beat her fists down on the desk in a wild rage of despair.

There were sounds outside. Footsteps, shouting, arguments in Italian, Anthea speaking in English ... Laura turned away from the window, hands over her ears, trying to shut out the noise—trying to wash away the misery. She threw the paperweight into a soft armchair. Damn the man! Why did she have to go and fall in love with such an unfeeling brute?

As she paced up and down the house gradually grew quiet. Then there was the sound of the launch and she imagined Anthea, her stepmother, being forcibly removed. What would the servants think? Oh, the *shame*! And suddenly Laura knew that she simply couldn't live here any more—not really because of what the servants would think, but because she knew the last shred of any feeling Karl might have had for her had now gone for ever.

Eleanora had seen to that. And now Laura realised just how ruthless Karl's mistress had been to get his undivided attention again. Tonio had been—what?— coerced, blackmailed? 'Have an amusing little holiday trying to seduce the new bride—and I will buy you a new powerboat.' She could almost hear the Contessa's dark, velvety tones. And if he hadn't succeeded—well, that didn't very much matter. As long as they were seen to be eloping—and how *kind* of Eleanora to rush over and try to stop them. And now, with sympathy and seemingly with the best of intentions, how easy for her to turn Karl's anger into loathing and contempt.

And she couldn't live with that, could she? That was far worse than merely taking second place. Her weary eyes rested on her mother's paintings, and for a moment she recalled Karl's adamant declaration that if she ever left him, he would search for her and bring her back. And with his connections ... But with Eleanora working on him, he wouldn't want to bring Laura back, would he? Unless he found out about the baby ...

But he mustn't find out—ever. So somehow she had to get away now, before she weakened again. Almost without noticing what she was doing, Laura wandered over to the window and watched the hired launch, only a speck now, bobbing towards the shore.

How could she escape? The boathouse was full of boats, but no one would let her take one out. She continued staring across the lake, hardly thinking, her mind confused, foggy ... A bit of a breeze was getting up; some little sailing boats were heeling over. Then she remembered Tonio's dinghy left on the beach.

CHAPTER TWELVE

Tonio's dinghy! Was it still on the beach? Laura knew she would never rest until she found out. Everything was quiet now—dared she go down to the beach and look? Cautiously she peeped out of the study door; the passage was empty, so she hurried along to the side door, sneaked outside, and found the steep, rocky way down to the shrubbery. At the bottom she fought her way through the bushes until she found the usual path. And it didn't take long to reach the beach after that.

It was there; still on its side, looking menacing, pointed-nosed, almost evil now that she knew she was going to have to sail it.

But suppose Karl remembered it was here, and moved it? Yet that was a chance she was going to have to take. She dared not leave until evening; perhaps if she locked herself in her room, stayed where he knew her to be, then his mind wouldn't start to wander. Please let him forget how Tonio had sailed here.

Luckily her plan worked. Karl kept out of her way all day; secure in the knowledge that she was upstairs— safe. The day dragged on and on. Her last day. The weather was cloudy, rainy with a stiff breeze she could have done without. Finally eight o'clock came and she judged it time to go. A last look round. Check passport, credit cards, money, cheque book. Her two nylon roll bags had been packed since last night. She took a deep breath to try and rid herself of this dreadful sick feeling. Standing in the middle of the room, she suddenly caught sight of herself in the mirror, and it wasn't Laura Rievenbeck staring back at her, but the old Laura, the student, in jeans and cotton-knit sweater, with an anorak over the top, and soft leather lace-ups in bright pillar-box red. All she needed to complete the picture were her paintbox and easel.

Cautiously, not daring to leave until it was nearly dark, Laura slipped out on to the landing, pulling the bags out after her, and locking the door again. She slipped the key into her pocket. She had left the light on in her room, and the radio playing . . . please don't let anyone discover she had gone until morning.

She crept along the landing and down the back stairs, praying she wouldn't meet any of the servants on the way up. There were sounds coming from the kitchen—pity she had never got round to telling Karl how hot it was in there. And thank goodness it sounded as if they were still busy preparing supper. Perhaps Karl had guests . . . one guest? She didn't want to think about that. From tomorrow he could have any guest he pleased, she would have given up her right to question such matters. Funny how it always came down to 'right'. Someone's right over another. Why did it have to be like that? Why couldn't people share the precious time together without dominating—without owning? Or was a very special *commitment* what life was all about?

Laura's face was grim as she let herself out of the side door. Possession or commitment, what did any of it matter to her? From now on she would let no man possess her—neither would she commit herself to any man again.

She had forgotten the torch. Damn! But somehow she scrambled down the rocks, stumbled along to the path, and finally reached the beach.

It was still there. No one had found it, and she stared at the dinghy, feeling sick again. It was going to take quite a bit of handling for someone as inexperienced as herself in this murky weather. It had stopped raining again, thank goodness, but she could only just make out the lights of the little town across the water. Suppose the rain obscured them completely? But this wasn't the time for a rich imagination. Laura dumped her bags in the boat, followed by her socks and shoes; then she rolled up her jeans, hoisted the sail, and started pushing the dinghy out.

Only it was quite heavy without Tonio's help, and it made a dreadful scrapy noise on the damp shingle. But at last it was afloat, and no one seemed to have heard. She scrambled on board, having to sit down smartly so as not to tip the whole thing over.

Phew! She sat for a moment, trying to remember how everything worked. She stowed her bags out of the way under a seat, and decided to keep her shoes and socks off because her feet were bound to get wet again at the other end.

The mainsail rope was loose, only they didn't call them sails, did they? *Sheet*, that was it. Well, the mainsheet was flopping about and she knew she had to pull it through that cleat ... then the wind would take them, which might be better than hanging around here because the lake was getting a bit lumpy with the wind—and there were those rocks over there ... So she kept the boom where it was, pulled in the sheet and fastened it in the cleat ... help, the tiller had disappeared, why had she left it until it was dark? No, it was all right, it had just swung over to the other side. So she pulled the tiller amidships and the nose, no— *bow*—pointed out of the little bay. Only then there was a creak and a flapping of sail, and—oh dear, the wind was on the wrong side now and the boom was going to crash over ...

Laura ducked in time and spent the next couple of minutes sorting out a jumble of ropes, most of which seemed to have become tangled with a pair of oars.

With her heart banging and her mouth dry with tension, she at last had everything in some kind of order, what a blessing Tonio had taken her out for that short trip and she could more or less remember how everything worked. Now they were moving, not quickly, because she hadn't trimmed the sail finely enough to gather any speed, but there was no way she was going to risk a forty-five-degree dash for the shore at ninety miles an hour!

It was a nightmare, and all Laura could do was to sit

in the stern with one hand on the tiller and the other
clutching the mainsheet, ready to whip it out of the
cleat if a sudden squall should threaten to push them
over. And because they weren't going fast, the little
boat seemed to ride every wave up and down, dropping
into the sharp little troughs and sending back a fine,
soaking spray. Laura set her teeth as her bottom
banged down on the hard wooden slats again. She was
bracing herself with a foot up on the opposite seat. And
there was nothing she could do except sit there and
somehow sail out of the little bay and into the wide
open expanse of the lake.

Just once she turned round and glanced back at the
lights of the villa. For a moment her eyes blurred with
tears, but she tried to tell herself it was the spray.

How long had she been out here, everything banging
and crashing about—hardly seeming to get anywhere?
In fact, the lights of Montiferno looked farther away—
or was it low cloud playing tricks?

But after another half hour, Laura knew it wasn't her
imagination. It was raining again, but the cloud wasn't
that low, and the patch of town lights was getting
smaller. Which must mean that the wind was sending
her sideways—crablike—so that if she was going to
make headway she would have to haul in the sail—get a
bit of a move on, probably tack . . .

The night went on for ever. It wouldn't surprise her
to learn that it was past midnight. Back and forth,
zigzagging towards the lights, the rain and spray
soaking her . . . the wind a dark devil sending squalls
that made her loosen the mainsheet in fright . . . which
meant she was probably drifting right back to the
beginning again. There was water in the bottom of the
boat now, so that her feet were freezing and every time
she changed position she slipped and banged her bare
toes. But at least the boom hadn't crashed across and
knocked her out. Well—not yet!

Only all this was really too much even for Laura's
sense of humour. The night went on and on, and she

could hardly see the lights at all now, and she didn't
have the faintest idea where Karl's island was. She was
so tired ... and she didn't know what to do. And the
waves were getting worse. But luckily she had found an
old plastic bucket, so if it came to a question of bailing
out ... And it wasn't long afterwards that she realised
things were getting pretty bad by any standards, let
alone her own! It was really blowing now, all the time,
not just when it rained. The sail was her main worry; it
kept flapping and banging one moment, and then filling
with wind and threatening to capsize the boat a
moment later. It gradually dawned on her that she was
going to have to take the sail down. The thought made
her feel sick—but if she was going to have to do it, it
might as well be now ... So she edged her way forward,
letting go of the tiller, crouching so that if the boom
crashed over, it wouldn't hit her into the water ...

At last she found the rope made fast at the bottom of
the mast, and her fingers were cold and stiff, and she
was shaking as she undid it and tried to lower the sail
slowly ... But it came crashing down, half falling into
the water, and she was certain it would capsize the little
dinghy. So she hauled it aboard frantically, and now
she was as wet as it was; a stiff blue and white tangle in
the bows, and somehow she found the oars and started
rowing ... with the tiller lashed amidships by a length
of rope.

It wasn't any good. She couldn't see the mountains,
or *any* lights, and the night was filled with crashing and
banging, and the interminable clang, clang of halliards
against the metal mast. The rudder rocked crazily out
of control as the rope around the tiller kept coming
undone ... All around her black sky, black waves,
black water in her face ...

For the hundredth time Laura began bailing out
again. How long could she go on? For all she knew any
moment they would go aground on rocks, or capsize,
and the lake was deep, very deep—and she was furious
with her inability to cope. Furious at not being strong

and capable and experienced. Why did the weather have
to be so foul? Then through her rage and fury she felt
the beginnings of real fear—and that was when the
brilliant, dazzling, *unbelievable* spotlight hit her.

In two minutes her terror was over. Blinded, holding
up her arm to keep the light out of her eyes, through
the rain and wind, she finally heard the heavy ticking-
over of a big engine. Someone was shouting her name—
and then there was a big boat alongside, it seemed to
tower over her . . . and someone was telling her to catch
a line . . . it was Karl.

Somehow he got her off the dinghy. For a moment
the two boats had bumped together and she had been
terrified as the dinghy had lurched away . . . She stood
up, clinging to the mast, rain and spray soaking her.
Then Karl was leaning over the rails reaching down for
her. She caught his hand, then he grabbed her wrist.

'Let go! Let go of the mast!' he shouted; only if she
did that and his grip slipped . . . *'Let go!'* he roared
again, and there was a mixture of anger and authority
in his voice—and really there was nothing else she could
do . . .

Then she was being dragged up by her wrists, her arms,
and at last Karl had an arm around her waist. And now
she was clinging on to him, banging her knee as he lifted
her over the rail . . . And it was all right, she was safe
. . . and she was clinging on to him and nothing else
mattered except that Karl was here. For a while tonight
she had thought never to see him again. Her grip
tightened as the deck heaved beneath their feet, and
now he was stroking her hair, murmuring something
she couldn't hear, and then the sound of the engine
grew louder as someone put it into 'ahead' and they
began moving.

'Come below.' Karl half led, half carried her into the
cabin, and at last she realised they were in his forty-foot
cruiser. No wonder it had seemed so big. He put a
blanket round her as her knees gave way and she sank
into a seat. She was shivering, wiping her face with hands

equally wet. And she was shaking, shaking uncontrollably. Now he was putting a glass in her hands. It was brandy, and she didn't like neat brandy.

'Drink it.'

At last she glanced up at his strong, severe, unreadable face.

'Drink it,' he said again, then he turned away and went to pour one for himself.

So Laura gulped it down, knowing it would probably do her good, but realising that the cabin was gradually filling with tension, aware that Karl's fear for her safety was turning into anger.

'Why?' He turned back to her, lightly balanced against the steady rise and fall of the cruiser, although it rode the short choppy waves far more easily than the dinghy. 'You could have been killed! You can hardly swim—the lake is dangerous even in calm weather. I have told everyone that you must never go out alone . . .' He put down his glass and strode over to her, bending down and taking her firmly by the shoulders. 'I have been out of my mind!' and then he lapsed into a fluid torrent of what sounded like a mixture of Italian and German; his eyes blue, hard, dominant, his voice angry, harsh, emotional . . . his whole body crouched in an attitude of latent aggression, as if at the slightest move from Laura he would be ready to spring.

'I didn't know it was going to be so rough,' she said in a shaky voice, and Karl's face changed subtly, as if his rage had turned inwards. He put her empty glass on the floor, then pulled her into a tight, fierce embrace, letting her cling to him again, burrowing her face into the strong, hard chest. And they stayed there, the motion of the boat rocking them together, until the cruiser came alongside the jetty and Laura realised they were home.

All was confusion and turmoil as Karl carried her ashore. The house, terrace and jetty were ablaze with lights. Bruno and his wife were rushing about; in the hall someone was phoning the police and telling them

she was safe . . . And Laura felt so ashamed and didn't
know where to look. But soon she was being carried
upstairs to her bedroom, and there was an awkward
moment when she saw with horror that the lock of her
door had been shattered. She looked at Karl, but he
said nothing, his face grim as he manoeuvred her
through the door and closed it purposefully behind him.

'You must get out of those wet things, have a hot
shower,' he began.

'I can manage . . .'

But he took no notice, unwrapping her blanket,
helping her out of her soaking things, carrying her
through to the shower . . . Then leaving her to go and
get some fresh towels.

While he had gone, she heard the phone ring beside
her bed, and he answered with a simple 'yes', then 'no'.
And then he came back to the bathroom, just as she
was beginning to dry herself with an old towel, and
began drying her back, her arms, all over her body, and
somehow it was an agony of joy and pain; the stong
hands familiar, intimate, drawing their own response.
Yet his manner continued to be cold, remote, brusque,
as if she had been nothing more interesting than a wet,
pitiful puppy.

'There's no need . . .' she tried again, brushing him
away, and he went to find her a warm dressing gown.
At last she was respectable, and came back into her
bedroom rubbing her wet hair with a towel.

Karl was sitting in the chair, waiting for her, pointing
towards a mug of hot cocoa and some biscuits that had
been brought up for her. She wasn't surprised; funny
how you soon become used to the attention of superior
servants. But it wasn't her world . . . she didn't belong
. . . And as she sipped her hot drink, Karl picked up her
discarded towel and began rubbing his own wet hair.
For the first time Laura realised how dreadful he
looked. His jeans were tight, old, she didn't know he
possessed such a pair, and they were wet from the knees
downwards. His feet were bare—*bare*—as if he hadn't

had time to dress properly, and the sweater was navy
blue, knitted in the Guernsey style; he looked tough,
rough, but as he threw the towel into a corner and
looked across the room at her, it was his face that dealt
the most shattering blow. Now, in the proper light, she
could see heavy, dark smudges under his eyes, the lines
of his face were taut and narrow, and the shadow of an
early morning beard gave him an earthiness that she
found strangely exciting.

No, she mustn't think about him like that any more.
Maybe he had saved her tonight, but that didn't really
alter anything between them. He was still standing
there, waiting for her to speak, his eyes shrewd, searing,
tearing down deep in her soul. She gulped and put the
mug back on the dressing table. 'I suppose you're
waiting for some explanation,' she began.

'I don't think an explanation is necessary,' he said,
with all the icy, aristocratic pride. 'You obviously
intended keeping your assignation with de Vito,
whatever the cost.' He swiftly crossed the room, rage
flashing in his eyes as he visualised her infidelity. And it
was in those eyes that she saw the words, 'You are my
wife and I shall never let you leave me for another man.
I shall keep you here by force if necessary', and
although he didn't actually say the words, both of them
knew what was in his mind. His whole body throbbed
with the undisguised rage of the Rievenbeck generations,
and she suddenly remembered those five brothers who
had held out against an army for six months . . .

'Go on—say it! I know what you're thinking,' she
said, anger, desperation and a dreadful hurt flooding
up inside. 'But you can't keep me locked up for ever.
One day I'll escape.' She broke off suddenly because
he was just standing there, tall and disturbed, staring
at her—frowning. Yet his eyes were full of a terrible
sadness . . .

'What—are we doing to each other?' he said in his
husky, fractured accent. Then he closed his eyes, turned
away, stretched himself, then wearily rubbed the back

of his neck. 'What can Tonio de Vito give you that I cannot?'

Laura was momentarily nonplussed and she bit her lip, glad that he had turned away and couldn't see her face. But then a sort of exasperated anger wiped out her other feelings, at Karl's continued insistence on thinking the worst of her.

'I'll tell you what Tonio can give me,' she said, and he turned back to her, his hands resting tiredly in the small of his back. 'He can give me my freedom.'

'Freedom?' Karl considered the word as if his command of English had suddenly vanished. 'But I thought you made a commitment to me.'

Now it was Laura who turned away, her face screwed up against the sudden rush of tears that threatened to break cover. 'We all make mistakes,' she whispered groggily.

'Ah.' A long pause, then, 'Maybe so.'

'And is that all you can say?' Laura responded, tears making her eyes bright with anger. 'You married me simply to get an heir—and with every intention of continuing your affair with Eleanora Ferrara—and you say *maybe* it was a mistake!'

'And that is worse than your indiscretion; marrying me for wealth and position and ensnaring young de Vito?'

'*Ensnaring young de Vito?*' she repeated incredulously. 'Birds of a feather, then, aren't we?'

Karl frowned at the unfamiliar colloquialism, but he obviously understood her meaning. 'You are wrong—I do not . . .' but he stopped at the sound of someone lightly tapping on the dressing room door. He cursed and went through to see who it was, and while he was gone Laura grabbed a tissue, blew her nose and dabbed quickly at her eyes.

'They thought you might be worried about these,' he said, coming back with the two nylon roll bags that she had stuffed under the dinghy seat. 'This is all they found.'

'That's all I took,' she sniffed.

'I see.' He didn't meet her eyes, the bags seemed to fascinate him. 'You do not take much—when you set out on this freedom.'

'I don't need much.'

He didn't reply for several moments. He was still holding the bags, they were wet and he didn't seem to know where to put them down. Laura wanted to snatch them from him in case ... But caution made her stay put ...

'I am prepared to forget about de Vito,' Karl said at last, speaking with little pauses between the words, as if they cost him a lot. But still he didn't look at her; still his eyes were riveted on the bags, and she could see his mind ticking over. What was in them? What did she consider of more importance than himself?

Panic made her jumpy. 'That's big of you,' she taunted, 'to forget about Tonio.' And at last he took his eyes off the wretched bags.

'At first I thought I could not,' he said quietly. 'This morning, *yesterday* morning, I thought I would kill him, and I thought everything was finished. But when I discovered you had gone,' he glanced at the broken door. 'When we realised what you had done, when we couldn't find you on the lake ... I knew then that I wanted you back under any circumstances.'

'Oh.' Laura wasn't quite sure how to take that. What was he offering her? Love? Or going back to playing second best? Oh, it wasn't fair! But what about the baby ...?

She chewed her bottom lip, playing for time, unsure what to do. 'And you expect me to forget about—her?'

He looked strangely enigmatic. 'Could you?' was all he said.

'I don't know.' She turned away again. Heavens, didn't he know she could forgive him anything? Then, in the dressing table mirror, she saw him frowning at the bags still in his hands, and he put one down and began unzipping the other. Oh no!

'Give that to me.' Laura spun round, scrambling across the bed to get at him. 'You've no right to look in there—they're my things!' but it was too late, and fired by her sudden suspicious concern, Karl tipped the contents of the roll bag into the middle of the bed. And oh, why did he have to choose *that* bag? 'Go away!' Laura tried to scrape everything into a disguising heap. 'You shouldn't have done that,' she sobbed, 'it's private.' But he was catching her hands, stopping her from hiding everything, and they both gazed down at the few tee-shirts and sweaters, hardly noticing them from the jumble of all the other bits and pieces.

Karl was still frowning, holding her away with one hand as he began sifting through her treasure trove.

'Stop it, you mustn't!' Near to tears, squirming and trying to wriggle free, all Laura could do was to watch his amazement turn into incredulity. Everything was there—*everything*. Theatre tickets, programmes from plays and concerts they had attended together. A champagne cork, the menu from that little bistro in Paris where they had gone the evening before their wedding. Tickets of a boat trip up the Seine. Photographs . . . a wild flower Karl had given her when they had climbed up to the ruined castle at les Andelys. All his letters sent to her in Paris when he was off on his trips . . . and the postcards too. Every little precious memento had gone into her bag because they were to be all she would have left of him.

'I don't understand,' he muttered. 'What does this mean, Laura?'

'If you don't know, why should I tell you?' she said, breaking free as his grip slackened, and beginning to scrape everything back into the bag.

He stopped her, his hands firm on her shoulders, his eyes bright. 'Tell me,' he insisted. 'I want to hear it from you,' and at last all her love was choking her and she broke down completely, clinging to him, her words stiff and halting, smothered against his chest.

He prised her from him. 'Say that again,' he said.

Laura sniffed and glared at him. 'I said—I loved you,'
and he closed his eyes, breathing deeply . . . 'And now I
suppose you're satisfied,' she said, 'but you needn't
worry, because I'll manage . . .' but she couldn't say any
more because his lips had closed over hers and she was
being kissed—and kissed. And now he was picking her up
and carrying her around to the uncluttered side of the bed.

'What are you doing?' she said, as he quite clearly
deposited her on the bed. 'You're mad—you don't love
me . . .' But now he was on top of her, trapping her, his
weight pressing her into the quilt and pillows.

'You aren't having an affair with Eleanora's brother,
are you?' he whispered, switching off the bedside light
that was glaring in her eyes. 'Are you?' he prompted,
and reluctantly she shook her head. 'Then where was he
taking you? Why did you want to run away?'

'He wasn't taking me anywhere——' She paused as
Karl brushed a curl, flattened by tears, off the side of
her face.

'I must have made you very unhappy,' he said, and
there was an undisguised catch in his voice; in the dim
glow from the other bedside light, she saw the deep blue
of his eyes fill with a private agony.

For a moment she didn't know what to say.
Unhappy? Oh, yes. But how to tell him of the exquisite
joy? And as her silence continued he rolled off her
slightly and undid her robe, sliding a warm, sensuous
hand over her breast, her stomach, and down the long,
smooth length of her thighs.

'We have to make it work, don't we?' he said,
burying his face in her body's voluptuous softness. 'For
our own peace of mind—for our sanity. And if you love
me . . .' he raised his head again, his eyes searching her
own, 'then where is the problem?' He continued
caressing her body, brushing the other side of the robe
out of the way, feasting on every sensitive line, curve
and mound. Suddenly his eyes snapped shut, but the
uncalled-for images didn't go away. 'But why did de
Vito say you were eloping?' his jealousy persisted.

Laura stared up at him. 'He didn't say we were eloping.' Her voice was still and quiet, almost unemotional, the words hanging in the air like frozen dreams.

Karl gave a funny, puzzled little laugh and was obviously going to disagree, then he frowned and she knew he was remembering that dreadful scene on the beach with Eleanora saying, *'It is all my fault—thank God we have arrived in time!'*

Karl was stunned. She saw doubt, incredulity and anger cross the planes of his face. Then he rolled off her and lay on his back staring at the ceiling. 'What has Eleanora been saying to you?' And to show the fury in his voice wasn't directed at Laura, he covered her hands and smoothed her palm with a caressing thumb.

'Eleanora doesn't say—she intimates. *Suggests*,' Laura added, seeing his tired frown. 'She gave the impression that you and she had planned it—planned to marry *anyone*. And that you intended returning to her after a couple of months . . .'

'And you believed all this?' His remarks were still addressed to the ceiling.

'Why not? It made sense. We hardly knew each other—and she's . . .'

He gave her hand a squeeze. 'Go on.'

Laura swallowed. 'She's—oh, *part* of all this, isn't she?'

'Part of what?' Karl rolled on to his side again, propping himself up on one elbow.

She sighed. 'Well, she's—used to this kind of life—*your* kind of people. *I* couldn't have organised that party.'

'Then why bother with it?' he interrupted.

'Because it's traditional—expected.'

He looked puzzled. '*I* did not expect.' He shrugged. 'I thought at Christmas or New Year, perhaps, when you had got to know my friends, I thought maybe then we could have a party . . .'

Laura sighed again. 'I wish you'd said.'

'You did not ask.'

'No, I didn't, did I?'

They kissed.

'And do you still believe that I resumed my affair with Eleanora?'

'You were kissing her at the fireworks . . .'

He shook his head. 'She was kissing me—there's a difference.'

Laura nodded. 'But you went to see her in Rome, after we got engaged.'

'It was only right that she be the first to know,' and when she looked uncertain, he went on. 'Ten years is a long time, darling, and I could not have her find out from someone else.'

'No.' Laura smoothed his cheek. 'But she was always *here*—always around you, and you didn't seem to mind.'

'I thought she was here helping you. You seemed to like her company—and I was having to spend so much time away. You see,' he smiled quizzically, 'I thought you were being very adult about my past—accepting Eleanora, realising that our love was strong enough to overcome any unusual situation.'

'Is—that how you felt?' Laura muttered.

'Of course.' He sighed, a little cross with himself perhaps. 'You see, I *thought* you had fitted in so well. You got on well with Bruno and his wife—and the kitchen staff didn't walk out.'

'Talking about the kitchen,' she interrupted, 'have you been down there lately?'

He looked slightly amazed. 'No, I don't believe I have.'

'I thought not. Karl, it's dreadfully hot down there—they need air-conditioning . . .' but she broke off because he was laughing.

'And you say you don't fit in? My darling, if you say they need air-conditioning, then that is what they shall have.' He was suddenly serious again. 'As long as you stay here to see the work completed.'

'I think I'd like to stay a bit longer than that,' Laura whispered.

'You are unbelievable,' he said. 'I have never loved any woman as I love you.' He bent and kissed her again. 'Not like this . . .'

'Oh,' was all she could think of saying, but deep inside there was a starburst of hope, love and joy.

'You see, it all happened in Paris,' he began, rolling on to his back again and taking her with him. 'Did I ever tell you about Paris?' She opened her mouth to speak, gazing down at him and allowing all her love to shine in her eyes. But he was silencing her with a firm finger across her mouth. 'I met this crazy, incredible art student in Paris,' his eyes flashed with the memory. 'She wore tight jeans and a scruffy smock, and she had masses of blonde bubbly hair, shorter than yours. And one day she smiled across a table at me, and I fell in love with her—I was so surprised I put three teaspoons of sugar in my coffee. It was undrinkable. What's the matter, darling? Why are you laughing?'

'Oh, it doesn't matter,' she said, remembering it had been the same sugar episode that had made her fall in love with him. But she wouldn't tell him, not yet. Today the memory was all his. 'You're mad,' she said instead, 'to fall in love with a little nobody like me. Look at the trouble I've given you already.'

'Never say that.' He was suddenly very serious indeed. 'But I was worse than mad, because I had forgotten how young you are. It was wrong of me to have expected you to accept Eleanora . . . and believe me, darling, I had no idea what she was doing to you.'

'Don't let's talk about her.' Suddenly the grand Contessa didn't matter any more, because all Karl's love was wrapped up with her on this bed. Then she suddenly remembered her stepmother. 'I didn't give Anthea any money—it didn't seem right,' she said.

He smoothed her hair. 'We will talk of her later—maybe we can do something . . .' and as the grey, misty morning light crept through the curtains they lay quietly together, Laura nestling on his shoulder, Karl gently smoothing her hair ... too tired to undress and get into bed. Gradually she was consumed with an overwhelming surge of peace, of coming home, of suddenly belonging—of feeling part of the family. Family! Oh!

'Karl ...'

'Yes, *liebling*?'

Laura struggled up from his arms, now that the moment had come she felt breathless, nervous; *please* let him want this for all the right reasons—please let it show in his eyes.

'Laura, what is the matter?' and then without knowing why, he seemed to catch her excitement, and the corners of his sensuous mouth lifted, and his lovely sexy accent purred. 'What are you trying to tell me? Is it about your painting? Do you wish to resume your studies? I have already attended to it,' he continued, brushing aside her wish for him to stop. 'I have already found an artist in Milano. We could both live each weekday in town. He is good. You will like to attend his classes ...'

'No,' she interrupted, impatient to share the news. 'Not yet, anyway,' and when he looked surprised, she gave him a shy, radiant, unbelievably sort of smile, and said. 'The lessons will have to wait for a while, because I—I *think* I've got something to tell you ...'

FREE-an exclusive Anne Mather title, MELTING FIRE

At Mills & Boon we value very highly the opinion of our readers. What <u>you</u> tell us about what you like in romantic reading is important to us.

So if you will tell us which Mills & Boon romance you have most enjoyed reading lately, we will send you a copy of MELTING FIRE by Anne Mather – absolutely FREE.

There are no snags, no hidden charges. It's absolutely FREE.

Just send us your answer to our question, and help us to bring you the best in romantic reading.

CLAIM YOUR FREE BOOK NOW

Simply fill in details below, cut out and post to: Mills & Boon Reader Service, FREEPOST, P.O. Box 236, Croydon, Surrey CR9 9EL.

The Mills & Boon story I have most enjoyed during the past 6 months is:

TITLE _____

AUTHOR_____ BLOCK LETTERS, PLEASE

NAME (Mrs/Miss) _____ EP4

ADDRESS _____

_____ POST CODE _____

Offer restricted to ONE Free Book a year per household. Applies only in U.K. and Eire.
CUT OUT AND POST TODAY – NO STAMP NEEDED

Mills & Boon
the rose of romance